BIG FISH

BIG FISH

Jon Gower

GWASG CARREG GWALCH

ISBN: 0-86381-619-3

Cover design: John Gillett

Published with the aid of the Arts Council of Wales.

First published in 2000 by
Gwasg Carreg Gwalch, 12 Iard yr Orsaf, Llanrwst, Wales LL26 0EH
☎ 01492 642031   🖷 01492 641502
✆ books@carreg-gwalch.co.uk   Website: www.carreg-gwalch.co.uk

Contents

Acknowledgements

'Sticca' was commissioned by the Southern Arts Touring Exhibition Service to accompany the show called 'Sticks' and appeared in the book of the same name. 'Turning Into Papa', 'The Dean's Last Day', The Secret of Growing Old' and 'Eight Life Cat' have appeared in Cambrensis; 'Bad Eating' and 'Teeth' were previously published in the New Welsh Review. 'Change on the Way' appeared in Merlin. Thanks to the editors of all three magazines.

Many of the stories in this book were written during a frenetic three months funded by a bursary from the Arts Council of Wales which is gratefully acknowledged.

Huge thanks to Stevie Davies for boundless encouragement and for her attentive editing of the collection, to Professor M. Wynn Thomas of Swansea University for reading the tales and kindly pointing out various flaws and failings and to Myrddin ap Dafydd at Gwasg Carreg Gwalch for his faith and support. Thanks also to John Gillett, a good friend, for the cover design. Diolch yn fawr iawn.

Big Fish

Brog Davies didn't hate his brother Stig, who was in America. He did, on the other hand, envy him his extraordinary luck, the emotion powerful enough to turn Brog all shades of green, from malachite to moss. He also envied Stig his name. He thought it much better than Brog.

Stig had luck which seemed on tap, drawn from some underground reserve which stored luck much as Texan oil wells contain their lakes of black gold.

Take the time Stig went sightseeing around the FBI headquarters in Washington. On being shown mugshots of the current Top Ten Most Wanted Men, he recognised one of them. Manuelo Suarez was the lodger who was living in his basement flat. That very evening a SWAT team burst down the door and caught the major-league drugs' dealer with his pants down in the company of a hooker dressed as a ballerina. This netted Stig a big reward.

Another time he was standing on a sidewalk on just the right spot to break the fall of a suicide jumper who then fell in love with him. Ulrika was a beautiful and gifted artist who would often regale visitors in their Manhattan flat – right next door to Woody Allen – how she landed on Stig from thirteen storeys up without causing more harm than might a brush of a dove's wing. Luck in enormous measure, Stig.

Stig number-crunched for a living, working executive hours in a blue plexiglass skyscraper. He played entire monetary systems off against each other, reserving a buck or three for himself.

Brog, meanwhile, lived in his Forestry Commission tied-house in the bowels of a dank Welsh wood where he spent many a hunched hour brooding over the colour postcards and photographs as they arrived. Ulrika and Stig in Acapulco. Their vacation, six months later, in Samarkand. Their beach home in Malibu, their penthouse in Los Angeles, their New York apartment with the telescope for watching joggers in Central Park below. There were times Brog drew moustaches on the two of them, a schoolboy defacing. But on dark days, when depression as grey as November mist seeped under the doors and insinuated itself through invisible cracks in the window frames, he went further. He mutilated the images of them, taking a sharp pair of scissors and cutting round the eyes. This took their power away.

He would curse them as he drew the whetstone back and forth along the edge of his woodcutter's axe, honing it until it was sharp enough to cut transparent slivers from a bluebell stem.

'Y diawl lwcus. Fe gath gyd o'n lwc i.'

It wasn't entirely true that his brother had been given his share of luck as well, but the thought bruised him inside.

Brog worked out with his axe, piling logs for winter. This was his element – the spreading boughs, the leaf litter a duvet deep, badger haunt and nuthatch haven. Brog shinned up larches quicker than a red squirrel, found the huge untidy nests of goshawks, nibbled fly agaric mushrooms which brought on wild visions of saints and rattlesnakes, high peaks and Biblical apocalypse.

There were quiet days when he listened to the trees converse. Ashes arguing on a sibilance of wind. The oratory of oaks. One day, when the whizzing teeth of a chain saw blade cut through a wild service tree Brog heard a tree scream, a sound piercing as a sparrowhawk's cry.

And then, oh shit, Brog bought himself a ticket to fly.

Four days and four nights later, Stig woke in the night to hear the sound of his neighbour seemingly chopping wood in the dark. When he heard the sound of a tree creaking loudly he decided to check it out. His ornamental palm tree had crashed down plumb centre of the car port and smithereened his Aston Martin Lagonda. His beautiful treasure was sullied, beyond the skills of the best panel beater.

Brog booked himself into a motel. In the morning he caught a bus and checked out the orange haired rollerbladers on Venice boardwalk, listened to gangsta-rap on outsize ghetto-blasters and pootled around some shopping malls. There was one less palm tree in the land. He chuckled, even as he decided to stay on awhile.

The incident had left Ulrika nervous, positively wired. L.A. was no town to have intruders lurking in the back yard, so she took her platinum card down to a firm that proclaimed itself in the Yellow Pages to be 'The security firm intruders die for.'

The office was on Cincinnati, a couple of blocks short of her hairdressers. A woman with a nose like a hawk and accipitrine eyes to match looked up from a leather ledger.

'Mrs Davies, I presume? Our consultant Mr Kurzik is expecting you. Can I get you a drink? We have some hugely refreshing tamarind juice.'

'Sounds good,' said Ulrika, as she was led into an office that would have suited the topmost lawyer in the land, all oak panelling and signs of serious success.

'Intruders?' said the man behind the desk.

Ulrika Davies answered with a nod.

She agreed a suite of measures including a sniper with night sights, razor-wire concealed in swathes of jasmine, rottweiler back-up, visitor screening, new door locks and a personal bleeper each for the Davieses which could summon the sniper's mate at a lick. The mate was a black belt in four martial arts with a Thai-boxer high kick and a collection of Purple Hearts that proved his Vietnam valour a ball park removed from the ordinary. 'Tough as titanium' as Mr Kurzik put it.

After the attack on his car Stig had the same tingling feeling in his chest and shoulders he'd had the night his father passed away.

It had been a dark and treacherous night, the night riven by fork lightning, a perfect backdrop for a dying. The old growler had passed away with a sigh. As his face became a mask, the lips curling back into what, in life, would have signalled hostility, Stig realised he'd thoroughly loved him but had left the equipment for saying it back there somewhere in his childhood. Now, when he thought about the two remaining members of his family – mother, brother – he heard a sound like tree fibres being torn apart.

Brog, nursing a contemplative vodka martini in an Eritrean restaurant, had a blemmer of a plan for further devilment, an inspired prank that would really pull his brother's wire. A better plan even than the time he'd made fireworks using industrial explosives. That year nobody, but nobody had a display to rival his. And certainly no one else managed to make the dead at the local cemetery sit up straight in their casks. It was a bang fit for Armageddon.

Brog had to arrange for all of his bank balance to be wired over to the Chevy Chase. It took two days but Brog twiddled no thumbs as he waited for the money. He bought an industrial-size roll of copper wire and, with subterfuge, near enough a coiled mile of magnesium ribbon. He bought some iodine and some powdered aluminium. A mixture of the two, using water as the catalyst, explodes in searing seconds of whiteness and a plume of purple smoke. Brog liked the fact that it was water and not fire that triggered the reaction, a certain chemical elegance. His schoolboy obsession with science was paying dividends.

That night he climbed into a tree opposite Stig's house, training his binoculars on the bedroom window. As he watched, the shadow of his brother crossed the frame. Brog had to make sure that he could see the window from the nearby hill, one of the most famous places in the whole of America, iconic. it must cost them a fortune to own such a view. Then he went up the hill to check the alignment. They really had to see this.

The security firm had trained an infra-red camera on the man in the tree and sent two men around, but by the time they got

12

there he'd vanished into the night, probably disappearing down a nearby storm culvert which they would add to the circuit of their patrols.

Brog's climb was difficult, lots of loops and straddling, hanging upside down and digging his climbing irons into sheer sides. After he'd used up all the magnesium he set up a pipette full of water and a timing device then he made the call.

It was Stig who picked up the phone.

'Hello . . . '

'Brog, is that you?'

'Look out of the bedroom window,' said Brog, excitement dancing in his voice.

Stig looked up at the huge letters which spelled out the word 'HOLLYWOOD' to the denizens of Los Angeles below. But tonight they burned bright with a different message as loops of Brog's magnesium lit up the smoggy sky. An aurora borealis for La-la land.

'*Cymru am byth*' said the words which flared and fizzed and shot out white light with arc-lamp brightness. Wales for ever.

'What do you think of my handiwork?'

Stig was laughing a ripe laugh, the sound of exploding fruit.

'It's wonderful. Icono-bloody-clastic,' he opined through a widening grin.

'Sure thing, brawd. But listen, I'm really sorry about the car.'

There was a glacial silence.

'You?'

'Me.'

'Some things never change!' said Stig, laughing again, waves of familial love caressing his body as he listened to his brother's voice, even as he located his tiny figure waving from the hill.

'Brog's here,' said Stig, turning to his wife whose beauty was enhanced by a pale peach incandescence, magnesium light reflected.

She nestled her body against her husband's. A twinkling of blue lights moved across the base of the hill as police cars converged and a CNN news helicopter hovered over the hill, filming Brog who waved back with the wide eyed grin of an escaped lunatic.

It took a couple of days for Stig to post bail on his brother. The police officer gave Brog his brown paper bag full of possessions, a movie moment.

'Well, well, here am I, a man who could only dream of getting his face on the cover of 'Time' magazine and here you are . . . ' handing him the magazine. Brog stared out, a startled squirrel cornered by a marten. Inside there was a news story and piece of heavy duty analysis by Christopher Hitchens which described Brog as a man striking a blow against the tyranny of global American culture.

'I think the whole world's media are trying to get hold of you – there are a couple of hundred of them parked up outside – which is why we're going out the back way . . . '

A police car took them both home. On the way Stig said, 'I'm taking you out of here tomorrow . . . '

Stig drove them north.

'We're going to Montana.'

'I've never been in a road movie before,' said Brog earnestly, fiddling with the air-conditioning controls.

Brog looked at his brother, studied him. In profile he was like their father, the same determined jut of jaw, the fleshy ears, whorled like pink sea shells. This was the man he'd envied all these years and they were driving to Missoula. They stopped at a diner which Brog swore he'd seen depicted in a Norman Rockwell painting.

'I thought you didn't come within a sniff of art living in your shed in the backwoods,' said Stig, the teasing tone echoing twenty years ago, when they used to spend every waking moment together. It was the same tone that had once provoked Brog into catapulting over a high wall into a demented neighbour's house to snaffle some apples. Mr Groodle was rumoured to have a gun, which proved to be well founded when the old coot pebbledashed Brog's behind from a shotgun full of seedcorn. Stig had laughed like a hyena, even as their dad later teased them out of Brog's whimpering flesh with a sterilised sewing needle.

'What went wrong?' asked Stig as the waitress in a cheery gingham dress brought them two outsized mugs of industrial strength coffee.

'I think I realised you were carving up an unfair slice of dad's attention. You were the great try scorer at rugby, you were the bees' knees when it came to passing exams. Your success was, well, relentless.'

They took the road to Reno and Salt Lake City, headed north through Pocatello, Blackfoot and Idaho Falls. They did the wildlife tourist thing at Yellowstone Park and skirted the Bighorn mountains, their conversation now an intimate tapestry of recollection. Fujicolor skies widened. The Bitteroot range was seemingly flattened by the weight of rain clouds overhead as they entered Missoula.

Stig opened the boot of the car. He fitted together the parts of a pair of fishing rods, light and pliable as willow wands.

Daybreak was a silk swirl of red and dark blue rags of leftover night. Barn swallows scattergunned across the surface of the river. Stig and Brog felt primitive, wading in the shallows, alive to the pulse of the river.

'There's a legendary fish in one of those big pools up ahead. The old people round here call it the Spirit of Bright Water.'

'I'd be loathe to catch a fish like that. Sounds like bad luck,' said Brog.

'I've seen it in my dreams . . . '

Light lamped down on the river which coruscated with splinters and slivers of broken sun. The brothers ploshed upstream under a canopy of high pines.

Stig was quiet now, willing his very breath to fall silent. The fish knew he was coming. A flick of its wide tail sent it sharking into a deep trench under some tree roots.

'It's there,' mouthed Stig, his heart beat quickening as he strained to hear the pumping of the gills, to sense the trout's mind flashing with the panic of the event.

In the company of his brother.

Stig cast a favourite fly into the water – Halham Webber's button spinner. Brog moved into greener water a few hundred yards away, casting with an awkward action but still managing to drop the fake insect smack on target, a smooth pane of water between two riffles of busy water.

Brog gave Stig a thumbs-up as he caught his first fish, a wriggling midget of a thing which he set free immediately.

Stig waved cursorily before returning to the mental wrestle with the Spirit. The fish had settled down, its belly almost touching a litter of dead leaves leftover from last fall – a pool which even spring floods failed to churn and disturb.

The fish, wily but not workshy, saw the fly break the surface gravity of the water above. It caromed up out of the depths. At the moment of impact Stig's muscles tensed to take the strain.

The big trout flipped magnificently in the air and bellyflopped. Brog watched his brother stumble then regain his footing on some flat rocks and arc his body backwards as he played the fish, running the line, feeling the Spirit volunteering for defeat. But not yet. The fish thrashed in white water, it swam straight back at Stig, feeling the line slacken. This was its last struggle. Exhaustion set in, its dorsal fin flattened by defeat.

Brog watched his brother catching the legendary fish, the Spirit of Bright Water and felt pride well inside him. The fish, two men, high trees, the dance of a river.

Stig invited Brog to take the hook out the fish's mouth, set the timer and took a photograph of them standing there, men of the same seed.

'There's a huge demand for tree surgeons in Los Angeles nowadays,' said Stig.

'You don't say,' replied his brother with a bright laugh, lowering the plump fish into the shock of water.

'You don't say . . . '

Precisely a year later, a time scale redolent of one of those medieval tales where the knight returns from his quest a year to the day he left, news came through of the accident in the goldmine which leached a toxic cocktail into the river. The river banks ran silver with a thrashing of fish. The tide of chemicals left the waters as biologically dead as a sheet of tin.

That same day Brog's illness started and even now, when Stig looks at the photograph which draws the eye with the same power as a crucifix in a chancel, it reminds him how the past can percolate through to sour the present moment, life a slow, growing litany, learning to live without. And when the fax machine is quiet and the phone sits at rest, he can hear the plash of Brog's waders and then the film starts, the faintly faded home movie of memory and Stig sees him then, his deeply loved and impossibly missed brother, taking great aquatic strides, marching into a day animated by dapple light, going for the big one.

Look out, he's behind you!

My fears that I was being followed were so strong that, going into town, I almost stopped at my brother-in-law Talfryn's house to borrow his flick-knife. After all, round here a sword is a damned sight handier than a pen. Being a writer in Brynteg is a bloodsport, it really is. I almost borrowed Talfryn himself, seeing as the boy is a champion Thai boxer and a dab hand at street surveillance. But as it turned out I didn't need him. I executed a classic double feint, nipping in through the front door of Del's Diner, made my excuses as I barged through the kitchen and sharked out into the alley at a lick. It took no time at all to double back on myself, and it was executed skillfully enough to catch anyone unawares, but there just wasn't anyone. Just a woman with a pram, and a man with a scarf wrapped round his face who looked like a dodgy salesman in Marrakesh, or an extra from 'Lawrence of Arabia'. How I do love that film!

I took my pulse in the way taught me as a boy by mamgu. Now there was a useful grandmother for you. She taught us to swim, taught us to read maps and by the time my brother and I started primary school we knew the names of all the stars and all the capital cities in the world.

One blessed day the subject came up – 'Today children we are going to study the capital cities of the world'. You should have seen the faces of the rest of the class when I got going. Haggis had failed to name the capital of Ireland while Dic-Dic, who wasn't much good at anything, offered Adolf Hitler as the capital of Germany. When their miserable trickle of answers came to a full stop the teacher asked, 'Now does anyone else know any more capitals of the world?' and that was my green light and I was off, launching into the capitals of West Africa to begin with, mainly because of all the tongue twisters which I knew would impress them like mad. Even the teacher – whose name was Mrs Howells if memory serves me well – looked a little astonished when I trotted out such gems as 'the capital of Burkina Fasso is Ouagadougau and the capital of Togo is Lome'. She had to stop me half way through the States of America. I can still name the world's capitals, even if my list is a little bit behind the times.

Mamgu also taught us how to fight – which was almost a social skill where we lived. The other kids took the piss like mad, but we-did-not-deride-them-for-that. How were they to know that mamgu was a born fight trainer, a downright inspirational eighty-five year old whose own father had outclassed Jack Dempsey? Three rounds, on the deck.

Every night for four months she took us to the garage. We shadow-boxed and did a lot of skipping – maybe half an hour every night – and as we danced there on the spot, the ropes getting treacherous with every passing minute, she would read her magazines. 'Y Tyst'. 'Y Goleuad'. Dark, sulphurous chapel magazines. I bet she would have loved those churches in Virginia where they hug rattlesnakes and copperheads. Poisonous snakes galore. She would have really loved those. She had the right rhythm to avoid a snake – should it be foolish enough to strike at her. We knew the rhythm. It was the deep-down rhythm of the big fight. She taught us that before anything else. Right. Left. Right, right, left – and all this in Welsh mind – de-chwith-de, ball of foot, right, right and then – The Astonishing Uppercut.

I checked again. My pulse was still up, as if I'd run to Carno and back. I was twitchy, unsettled. There wasn't the least sign of my calming down so I slipped into the 'Lion' and dropped a 'Depth Charge' in the middle of my paranoia. For those of you who aren't cognoscenti of a good drink I'd better explain. To make a classic depth-charge you drop a schooner of Drambuie into a pint of dry cider. You hardly get to taste the 'Dram' during the first half pint and then – whammy! Lovely drink. Sophisticated.

Now that I was relaxed again – verging on dead cool – I left the 'Black' and sauntered out onto Main Street. Then I went down Brymbo hill and took the short cut through the park. Leaves were forming drifts by the side of the pond and there were some lovely specimens – lots of crinkled maples and bird cherry. On the lake, tufted duck plopped underwater, not pleased to see me. Some kids were turning a roundabout into a centrifuge, spinning faster and faster so they were all so scared and all so very happy.

I almost forgot about the tensions of the morning, but not quite. Every so often I'd stop and look around, until I felt rather stupid and tried to pull myself together. But there was one nagging thought.

Around here they call me the leech because I write and lots of people are worried that I'm going to put them in my books. Some worry that the Social Security will catch up with them because they're actually working in one of my novels when they shouldn't be. As if Social Security inspectors read novels! It's like living among tribesmen who are scared of your camera stealing their souls. I've certainly learned not to bring my notebook out in pubs anymore, after a steel erector called Terry, a trifle annoyed about the fact that I was busily transcribing the story he was telling his mate, had threatened to turn me into paste. Let's face it, it could be anyone following me.

That same afternoon I was attending evensong, but I couldn't concentrate on the glory, the uplift of the thing. Because a ridiculous bloke in the pew behind was hissing at me, insistently.

'Pssst! Hey you! The one with the face. You've got to get me out of this mess.'

Although I really, really didn't want to – what right had this man, this utter stranger – to interrupt me in the middle of the service – I half looked, then felt myself being pulled in.

I'd presumed his face to be puffy with booze, or fat, but with closer scrutiny it revealed itself to be just one amorphous mass of flesh, like pink putty. No nose. No eyes. No mouth. No nothing.

'What the . . .

But he headed my half-sentence off at the pass.

'I'll tell you what. I'm one of your characters, pal, from a perfectly infantile piece in a school magazine from way back. You probably don't remember so much as a phrase of it. Well, let me tell you something. You didn't have the common courtesy to give me any features, just this, which isn't very much at all. If it hadn't been for my wandering blindly into a Robin Cook novel – where they happened to need a male patient for an emergency tracheotomy – I wouldn't even be able to speak.'

He undid his silk cravat to show a partly healed stoma and a nifty little voicebox.

He crossed the two ends of the cravat and the pale disc of the man's face – or where his face should be – glistened in the dim light of the clerestory.

Panic rose in me like bile. I got to my feet and, awkwardly swinging myself along the aisle, accidentally kneed a supplicant old man in the ribs, winding him. I helped him to his seat and then, as if propelled by compressed air, I headed out through the side door. As I scooted out through the lych gate a naked man came towards me on all fours, pushed down as if by some invisible force from above, so that his body looked homunculoid. He looked up at me imploringly, but I passed him by, cleanly, then breaking into a canter, eager as hell to get away from the place.

Back in the house I cracked open a fresh bottle of Jack Daniels. There was a whiff of carbolic soap and a hint of brimstone in the air, as if mamgu had been in the room. That was the sort of Puritanical zeal she had, follow you back from the grave just to ensure you couldn't enjoy your sin. A woman and a half. And I was right. There on the sofa was the old lady – as if we hadn't buried her – what was it – fifteen years ago. She was knitting something which looked like a scarf.

And then she looked at me and said – and here I'll have to translate as we go along like they do in Strasbourg.

'*Beth ti'n neud da dy hunan dyddiau 'ma Iolo* – What are you doing with yourself nowadays Iolo?'

'*Sgrifennu straeon pan gallai.* Writing stories, when I can.'

'*Ond o'n ni'n meddwl dy fod ti'n mynd i fod yn ddoctor neu'n gyfreithiwr* – I thought you were going to be a doctor or a lawyer.'

'*Ces i ddim y graddau iawn* – I didn't get the right grades.'

She nodded – a stiff nod of disappointment with a hint of reproachment.

And then she said, '*Ma 'na bethau rwyt ti heb i gwneud* – there are things you've left undone' and with that she disappeared with that same dissolving effect you get in 'Star Trek' when they beam down to some dreadful planet or other. It took me by surprise I call tell you.

As I swilled another serious measure of the good stuff around in the glass, a movement out in the shrubbery caught my eye. I saw half a man, just a torso, dragging itself through a stand of lupins. Another of my monsters. I then understood. It all became clear to me. I saw, as if with total sight, what was going on here. I recognised the torso. I recognised the man from Lawrence of Arabia. And I'm sure if I read that school magazine article from way back I'd recognise the man-with-no-face. Mamgu had given me more than a broad hint. Everything I'd left half-written was coming back to me. What goes around was coming around.

If this was true, then even the next sentence I wrote could get me into trouble, into big trouble. I remembered the story I'd only just written in which my alter-ego was a hopeless junkie, Zonkoid George by name, a dumb fool who'd popped all the veins in his arms and was now pushing the syringe in between his toes. I didn't want him around, especially as I was going home tomorrow. My mother doesn't like people who drink even. God knows what she'd make of someone getting spaced on Panthium.

And then some other stories – all half-finished, some discarded – came flooding back to me. The one about the wolves which had escaped from a wildlife park somewhere in Cardigan. They were still out there somewhere, their senses sharp as sharp can be.

Or the story about the two bullets heading for the three members of my family and I have to choose which one to pull clear.

It took me two days to pull everything together. Box files stuffed with abandoned short stories came to light, and a kitchen drawer full of scraps of characterisation, odds and sods like that, and a third of a telly play about Julia Pastrana – the Gorilla Woman. Thirteen connected but totally ludicrous pieces about Mishima, half a thriller, and a vainglorious bid for the horror market called, I thought rather pithily, 'The Transplanter'. A load of baloney really. It really was.

I sat down at the table and poured another bourbon. I wasn't sure whether I should start with a bit of spare-part surgery out there in the middle of the lupins, conjure him up a fine pair of legs, or should I describe, down to the very last pore, a good face for the man in church. Slowly, I picked up my Newtown Rugby Football Club centenary biro, and began to write.

Trio Fascisti

The night they decided to kill the guy in the corner shop had a pale moon, full and sheeny as a woman's carrying belly, high up, so very high up over the roofscape.

'You wanna kill him?' asked Smiler, lighting a spliff.

'Course I do, pardner. Sure as daisy. Someone's got to go down, mun. Never to get up, mun. Let's just do it . . . '

'Mun. That's the word you were looking for. There's something lacking in ewer vo-cab-u-l-ary ma boy.'

Jocky one-handedly swung a baseball bat at them. He didn't want abuse. Not now. Not when he was chillin' out with a big turd of a joint.

Three brutalized young men, with lives behind them that would read like horror books. Nothing to live for. Nothing to look back on. That's as maybe but no excuse for strolling down, insouciant as can be, to Mr Khan's grocery and running a seven inch blade clean up through two ribs, puncturing a lung and leaving the man to die outside his own shop – squealing, pleading, this grandfather. His death was a rivulet of dark blood running across the chewing gum studded terrain of the pavement, deflecting the flow of it. A crowd of people, who would be forever numb, their emotions cauterised by the sight of the little man, gasping as a fish. The little man who, hail or sunshine piped up a 'How Do You Do' when you walked in the door. Lying there, gasping.

Three streets away the skins chortled to themselves. It had been a good laugh. Bostic said he could murder for a kebab, and as they had murdered felt a donner was owed them. Gristle meat in a wrap of sheep-fat probably too viscous even for the lipstick factory on the estate. Jocky punched Bostic's arm.

'A triumph.'

'A night with a difference.'

Smiler scowled, dragging on a Rothmans as if on an oxygen mask. The Asian guy had given him a choc-ice, years back. For free, on the hottest day of summer. For free for Chrissake! He pulled his lumber shirt around him like a doom. He was glad and relieved that Bostic it was who had done the deed. He couldn't have lived with himself. Probably couldn't now, anyway. He felt sorry for himself, and for how his soul had turned. He smoked the fag down to the filter, tried to smoke that even, the acrid taste cheering him. The gunky brown taste reflected the state of him better than a mirror would.

The police didn't need three guesses. They took a van and seventeen officers round to pick them up. They were down the pool hall.

When they arrived at the station they bounced Jocky down a flight of stairs, just to make him feel welcome. Bostic was as high as a kite. He'd sniffed some fire extinguishers before hitting the pool tables. And some E. His pupils didn't look right for speed. They weren't pin pricks of black. Anyway, it was more than they needed as an excuse for strip-searching him. Used some marigold gloves and a claw-hammer. Then they phoned his father, just to let him know where Bostic was, that he was safe.

Bostic was, they reckoned, the ringleader. He was the youngest (note not the only) Klan member in Pontcnwcwll. Frisking him fully and they find a knuckle-knife with the inscription 'Co . . . slicer' – the blade worn away and covered in caked blood. They pop it into a plastic bag and then relieve him of a pair of rice flails, also named, this time 'Mam' and 'Eyeburst'. In his house, that night, they find a collection of Nazi whotsits, with swastikas and pamphlets by John Tyndall and Martin Webster and a shelf of books which Smiler used to read to him, much as a mother reads to her child. Except it wasn't 'Pippi Longstocking'. Books heavy with the dreadful fug of smoke over Buchenwald. And 'Mein Kamf' in pictures.

Bostic can't read, but is coolly intelligent. A gaggle of prison shrinks could attest to that. He's done a deal of time for a man so young, what with the remand and all. He's a bugger at a Rorschach, forever finding the most wonderful images in the squidged ink-blot – and able to beat a lab rat to the middle of a maze. Thinks quick, if not too deep. He's done three stints in all, recently in Usk where they probed the septic side of his sexuality, the burstable boil of his drive. The love of submission. Evil's not a concept. Just another way of life.

Bostic got this romantic world-view from his dad who would keep him up late every night to watch films. Skin flicks his dad called them. Vulgar and exact. It messed up his brief school career. Staying up so late. To watch the scrummages of flesh, the ménages a trois and quatres and more, so much more, what with the double-ups and the contortionists. Dad especially liked films starring Wobbly Wenda, who seemed to Bostic to be way past her sell by date. He can remember a joke his dad used to say, time and time again. 'Why do porno films have those bloody awful soundtracks?' 'Dunno, dad.' 'So blind people know when to whack off as well.' Memory of a father. A father run over by a dustbin lorry as he staggered home after a major league bender at the Legion. The stuff of memories. The ambulance men scraping up the pulped bits of him with a shovel.

Seen-it-all sergeant Harry Baldry sat opposite Jocky. Interview Room Three. Walls tawny with nicotine and filled with idle-time graffiti.

'Why did you do it?'

'Full moon.'

'What?'

'Full moon. Influences people more 'an you think.'

'Is that your defence?'

'Just an observation, ya bloated pig.'

Baldry wondered how to engineer a death in custody.

The crowd which had gathered outside was simmering its way up to flash-point. They were mainly white. A surprise maybe. Maybe not. The crowd numbered two hundred, or more, and moved and shivered with an inner pulse, like a protozoan. Every so often a chant would go up. 'Hang em!' With the qualifier. 'High.' 'Bring out the three!' they shouted, with gusto enough.

Smiler was in his cell, listening to the Top Twenty on the radio the man from the Prison Visiting Service had brought him. The phone call had cost him his last ten pence piece. The goons had even refused him so much as a pot to piss in. He could hear the crowd outside giving voice to his name. He half-smiled and drifted into the techno-lull and beat of the number three hit single.

The skies crackled up with pent-up and phenomenal energies. Ball lightning had been sighted for the first time in living history. In Interview Room Four, three men were gathered – three policemen, three fathers. Baldry was saying he was sick to the gills with this stuff. The bastards were showing not a jot of remorse. The other two, Shepley and Sproat agreed. The white flashes outside lit up the purpose of their eyes. They decided to leave the van door open when they took the prisoners to the magistrates' court in the morning. Someone would be sure to try the handle – especially if someone was given the nod.

Norrie Bristol, the people's academic, had privileged access to prisoners. He was putting the finishing touches to a study that would prove, finally and beyond doubt, the link between on-screen and off-screen violence. He'd interviewed a thousand violent criminals, in police stations and holding bays and a couple of prisons. Like a Grand Tour of the seedier side.

He'd met the most resistance not because of what he was doing but where he was doing it. Everyone in Cardiff seemed to be cloyingly proud of the cosmopolitanism of the place, shored up by the longheld belief that the big town-small city didn't have the least hint of racism. Everybody getting on. All the way back. And now. In the small city-big town.

Somali women, like galleons in full sail, tall but not haughty, their cheekbones high and ribbed, like rigging for a drape of beauty. They beggared belief. And their grandfathers, stranded here when the sea-trades died down, telling tales of camels and nomads in the trapped-ness of their council flats. A business of Chinese who kept the casinos going late into the night and who retailed and sold and wholesaled by day, hard working as Syrian traders. Maltese taxi-drivers, their cabs done up like mobile shrines to the Virgin, filled with an incense of Woodbine smoke. Bangladeshi restaurateurs, their eyes seemingly tinged with turmeric, or a hint of turmeric. In-your-face West Indians, training to be Yardies; the less-in-your-face ones kind as angels, with tubes of ganga big as ear-trumpets glued to their lips and skanked up sound-systems pumping out 'Yellowman' and other dread sounds. Poles, forever exiled, and Nigerian students, hooked on mathematics.

The place is a mess of colour and diversity and a hotch-potch of tradition, a medley of religions singing different songs, and all getting on oh-so-very-well with the heart-of-gold Cardiffians.

Not so! Not so at all! Hold on just one minute there!

Consider, then, the taunts made, the bottles thrown, the jibes, the fate of waiters in curry-houses, their patrons urinating in broom cupboards, the sag bhajis hurled over wallpapered walls. And taunts galore. Slant eyes for the Chinese. Japanese children. Encouraged to remember Nagasaki. By seven year old co-pupils. The exotic flower of racial harmony nursing a maggot at its heart. And the broken headstones of Jewish cemeteries. And the toilet-cleaning jobs for the wise old whaling captain from Cape Verde. And the grim flats full of Old Africans. The mispelled daubs of racist graffiti in Riverside, Ely, Canton, Vic Park were testimony. But when the chicken-shit skins with their leering grins put a thirty two hole D.M. hard into an old man's skull, before slitting him like a pig there was no witness. Menace and the pompous princes of the motivelessly malign walked in their triumph on the streets. Walked in their own, radiant, unbridled triumph.

Professor Bristol, having spoken to the three young killers with their eyes of permafrost, understood now. He had a thousand people in a thousand people sample who'd turned to violence in a maelstrom of film and tv images. These last three, numbers 998, 999 and 1000 respectively, clinched it. John Hughes, aka Smiler, with his Shaun Hutson books, his pirate snuff movies and newspaper cuttings about political torture. Kevin Bremner Davies, aka Jocky, with his compulsion to watch Romero films over and over again. Night of the Living Dead. Return of the Living Dead. Like big screen versions of Stanley Spencer paintings, with buckets more gore and molten faces. Bristol knew he was on to a blockbuster. Better than Norman Mailer with his 'Executioner's Song' and on a much bigger canvas. He knew it would sell millions.

Smiler, Bostic and Jocky had breakfast together. Odd. Not usual police protocol. Certainly they were surprised it was so decent – a MacDonalds tray apiece with hash browns and a Sausage and Egg MacMuffin and two cups of coffee each with tiny pots of half cream and a pile of sugar sachets. There was even a ten pack of Bensons which they smoked in a smog of suspicion.

Now the first hairline cracks opened out on the masks of their composure. Something was up. Something was really up.

The van drove out through the electric gates of the compound and the crowd surged through the token blue line, banging on the sides of the van, an anger raking their faces like a searchlight. The One-Who-Knew the back door was unlocked yanked it open with a whoop.

There hadn't been a public dismemberment in these parts for a good few centuries but by the time the edge-of-frenzy crowd had finished with The Evil Three (as the 'Sun, the 'Star' and the Mirror had dubbed them – as if their headline writers were collectively feeling fatigued – couldn't be asked to do better) they might just as well have been strung between two top-of-the-range John Deere tractors and been ripped apart fibre by fibre, in a scattergunning of flying corpuscle. Intestines popped and it was blood-o-rama out there. The three policemen felt no remorse. They felt justice was being done.

The bloody event commandeered the Thursday news, clogged the channels, surfed the vast oceans of the airwaves, upsetting, angering, drawing heated condemnation and half-hearted explanation. Apart from Professor Bristol, who as soon as he was used by the BBC six o'clock news was bombarded with requests for interviews with CNN, the satellite services in Japan, cable, RTF, WTN, the works. His publishers reckoned that if he finished the book next week they'd have it in the shops in a month.

The 'Sun' won the front-page battle hands-down. Two words. 'Mob Rule.' And a photograph of faces contorted with hatred and the bloody head on a pole (the crowd wasn't satisfied with death, they wanted all the trimmings). There were outbursts of sympathetic violence. A National Front sympathiser in Rhyl was tarred and feathered. Skinheads had a lot of hassle wherever they were. Ffostrasol even. And Aberangell. Scarcely believe there were any that far upriver.

And then on the Friday a preacher man, interviewed on the local 'Red Dragon News' said 'I think it's time we prayed' and as if both bowed and released by the words people, the breadth and length of the big town – small city did exactly that. Old, musty and tired chapels with brimstone names such as Pisgah, Gerazim and Rehoboth threw open their doors to sunlight and air, after years of abandonment. In all the 'ist' churches Christian Scient-ist, Advent-ist, Pentecostal-ist and a charisma of others the crowds filled them so full that some had to hose down the congregations. Kyrie eleison, kyrie eleisons were repeated as mantras in hundreds of Anglican churches.

In supermarket aisles shoppers lay prostrate, next to the cold counter, next to the racks of tinned cat and dog food. The girls on the tills switched off their bar-code machines and let their heads hang. Workers downed tools – shovels, steering wheels, biros. Typewriters stopped clacking, cooking ceased as the message passed from lips to ears. Let us pray. It was repeated on the radio, played almost as a jingle by some jocks. Interrupting the music of car pools and lifts, of video showrooms and lounge-bars. Let us pray, it said. Let us pray they did. There had been enough bad time. Time to forgive, though not to forget. Not entirely. Strangers were invited into the homes of strangers and were encouraged to start learning the strange sounds of a foreign tongue. Glottal stops and clicks like Bushman. The sibilance of Arabic and all manner of high lilts and beautiful comings to earth. An invisible and utterly unrealized family hove into view, their faces drifting slowly into focus. And in Thornhill cemetery, one Wednesday morning, a young girl walked up to Smiler's grave and placed a small flower of forgiveness. Soon, so very soon, there would be more.

The Secret of Growing Old

On the day absolute love visited Lev Thomas he was feeling like the poor deluded bird in the proverb. You know the one. 'The sparrow flying behind the hawk thinks the hawk is fleeing.' Lev suffered delusions of grandeur substantial enough to take wing, get him up there, chasing hawks. He'd asked the doctor for a prescription to take care of it. Temazepam, any old knock out drop, but Old Doctor Frosty had told him to bugger off, said that Lev was mad enough without marzipan – which was dangerous stuff indeed. That's what the old coot said. Marzipan. What hope was there?

Being Friday, Lev had finished his last shift of the week at the chamois leather factory. As he walked through the factory gates he was wondering how many windows had been cleaned with the fruits of his labours, how many soapy wringings he'd engendered. A thousand? Two thousand?

The road across the common shimmered in a heat-haze. The fly-tippers had been busy on both roadsides, dumping carpets, dumping plastic carrier bags full of old tin cans and seven kinds of garden rubbish. Skylarks rose like miniature Harrier jump jets, executing perfect Vertical Take Off and Landing techniques above the Juncus rushes and clumps of couch grass.

Lev's thirst was at a premium when he arrived at the lounge bar of the 'Madagasgar Retreat' – a pub rather lacking in basic hygiene. The only people who'd enjoyed their brief stay were a crew dressed in bio-chemical warfare suits who'd stopped by on a day trip from Porton Down. They'd drunk beer through tubes. Peed through tubes as well, like cosmonauts.

The furniture was riveted to the floor to stop overenthusiasts throwing them out of the window, or at old age pensioners. But, like the sparrow, Lev could see things in a more convenient perspective. Standing at the bar was Terry Twist – a drinker of such conviction that it was rumoured he'd had his toes amputated so that he could stand nearer the bar. T.T. blew the froth from his thirteenth pint of the day and grunted a welcoming sound vaguely in Lev's direction.

At twenty six minutes past four the woman Lev would love more than any other walked in, bold as brass. His Juliet, his Helen, his Aretha Franklin (whose 'Say a Little Prayer' woke him every morning on the cassette radio). At twenty seven minutes past she straddled a bar stool, this woman called Noragh – a fifty-eight year old dedicated drinker with a liver the size of a kidney stone and a sporadic career in painting and decorating. She addressed Nugget, the barman, as if he were a long-lost friend.

'Nugsie, my old comrade in the battle ag'in the jitters, pour me a large jug of your frothiest. I have me one inferno of a thirst.'

She emptied the stein which Nugget produced from the darts' cupboard, like opening a drain. Noragh wiped her lips with the bib of her overalls, then winked at Lev who, with that one wink, fell in love as deep as a well. There were no cascading strings, no unspecific epiphany, but he went head over heels, tumbled in love with the strange woman, like a clown, like a clown tumbling.

Everything then seemed to follow a quasi-divine plan. Noragh dropped a ten-pence piece in the jukebox and up came that voice. Aretha! That gutsy passion. That voice of perfect register! And that song! That in-your-face emotion which always had Lev sailing his weep-ship over lost and hopeless seas.

Then Noragh bought him a drink.

'Nugsie,' she said, 'get this man a drink strong enough to bring him out of his coma . . . What's your name, flower?'

Lev thought of a smart-alec answer.

'If my name was that of a flower it would be fire-flout' remembering the wonderful list of flower-names he'd seen on his Auntie Lil's apron.

'What, a poppy?' asked Noragh, with the confidence of a tweedy botanist. If Lev was smitten before he was tragically doe-eyed now.

She then started reeling off wonders. Told him about the sixty thousand Avon ladies who work in Amazonia.

'In remote villages a dozen eggs gets you a Bart Simpson roll-on deodorant. Twenty pounds of flour gets you a bottle of cologne. In mining outposts a gram of gold buys you 'Crystal Splash' perfume.'

Lev recoiled from the weighty irony in her voice. He thought of the cluttered shelf in the bathroom back home, to where the Bart Simpson deodorant sat, a full bottle's worth of embarrassment.

She then surprised him out of his skin,

'Would you like to stay with me tonight?'

Lev had no experience in these matters, other than a brief explanation of sex in school. It was all crammed into one biology lesson, where the teacher twisted two artists' mannikins into such contortions that a leg snapped off.

After a long shift at the bar, they stumbled and fell and picked themselves up all the way back to Noragh's house. It was perched on a rickety terrace which involved climbing the Kilimanjaro steps, as they were known locally. By the time they'd negotiated the hundred and fifty steps they felt exhausted. On the way Noragh kept reeling out a ticker-tape of facts and figures. It was more than encyclopaedic.

'Did you know,' she asked, gripping the handrail like a crash victim learning to walk again, 'that there are nineteen million cells in every inch of human skin . . . and nineteen feet of blood vessels . . . and nineteen thousand sensory cells? In every inch, mind you!'

'Must have been one hell of a job counting them all,' said Lev, his mind stuffed full of figures. 'Do you reckon they actually found nineteen thousand whatsimucallit cells, or is it a case of trying to make a guess sound like exact science?'

'Lev, you're being far too profound for the hours after stop-tap. Kiss me.'

Lev attempted a clumsy Hollywood kiss. Michael Douglas and Demi Moore in 'Disclosure'. Open lipped, hot with steamy passion. His tongue felt the plastic of false teeth. They unclinched after a good ten-minute kiss, long enough for Lev to need his asthma inhaler at the end of it. He took a draught of the medicine deep down into his lungs.

As Noragh opened the door, she told him about a man called João de Barros. The keys slipped out of her grip. Half-kneeling, she continued her brief tale. The man was a Portuguese historian whose history of the Portuguese empire so pleased the king that he gave him a whole state in Brazil, a hundred and thirty thousand square miles of it.

'Would you believe it?' she asked, ushering him down the passage.

Noragh backed up all her stories with figures. She put the kettle on, while telling him about the hate mail Harriet Beecher Stowe got after 'Uncle Tom's Cabin' hit the shops. One of the parcels she received contained the ear of a slave, 'hell's teeth the ear of a slave,' she said and poured the tea while telling him without pause at all about bees and how they must visit two million flowers to make a one pound comb of honey. Lev was reeling, saturated with facts, unable to process any more.

'Listen,' said Lev. 'I'm suffering a bit from information anxiety. Too many things bombarding me at the same time. Can't we talk about something else?'

'O.K.' she said. 'Ask me a question. A real chancer. No holds barred. Whatever you ask I'll answer truthfully and fully.'

The question formed as if by magic on Lev's lips.

'What's it like to be old, Noragh?' The question you don't ask. You simply don't ask.

Noragh seemed unphased. An idea drifted across her eyes.

You could see it moving – right to left.

'I'll show you what ageing's like. Walk this way.'

She led him into the bedroom.

'Take your clothes off,' she said, dominatingly. Lev's heart took a little leap of apprehension, the rhythm of the heart's systole skipping half a beat.

'Everything?' he queried, taking off his trousers, his voice up an octave with nervousness.

'Keep your pants on if you're shy. But don't worry. This has nothing to do with sex. I haven't lured you here for a spot of Big Rudies.'

Lev stood there, awkwardly, in his underpants, while Noragh rummaged around in the bathroom, sounding like a bull in a china shop. She came out with an armful of bandages.

'Lie down, poppet. Take the weight off your feet.'

She wrapped bandages around his joints, tightly wrapping and binding. When Lev tried to stand up he could barely move a limb. Noragh then disappeared into the kitchen, coming back with a pile of old fashioned weights. She clipped some of them to the bandages with clothes pegs.

'These'll give you a sense of your muscles being weak. That happens as your body grows tired after all the years.'

Lev didn't feel at all foolish standing there, almost naked, wrapped in bits of bandage with weights hanging from various parts of him. Noragh was looking at him, fixedly. She was serious about this – the fixedness of her eye said so.

By the time she'd given him a pair of spectacles with crusty old lenses, scratched so badly they were almost opaque – as if someone had rubbed them with low grade emery paper – and then tied wads of paper squares cut from the Daily Mirror to his ears Lev was feeling quite edgy, as the world he knew got hazy and locomotion became a painful, tentative thing, one difficult step at a time. He was being given an out-of-focus glimpse of how things would be. How they really would be.

Noragh took him by the hand and stood him at the base of the bed. She sat on the edge and unclipped a stocking, rolled it down her leg. She took off all her clothes, one by one. Lev felt like Dustin Hoffman in 'The Graduate', watching Anne Bancroft.

She drew him down to her. 'Will you still love me tomorrow?' she crooned, her voice thin and beautiful as she rolled Lev's clumsy body over onto its side.

'I will,' said Lev, definite as can be, kissing her, kissing Noragh with all the tenderness he could, kissing her with his eighty year old or ninety year old lips, as if Noragh'd always be there.

Bessie Peak Rate

Unbeknown to her neighbours, Bessie Harries ran a thriving little cottage industry from her sunny kitchen. Unbeknown because illegal, Bessie ran a telephone sex service called 'Talk Erotic', taking as many as forty calls a day, in between peeling carrots, ironing, all that jam.

She'd started off her career as a listener, curiously enough, with The Samaritans, clocking up three, maybe four twelve hour shifts a week.

One night, against all the rules, she dashed, fast as her Metro would allow, to a man's house. She knew, she just knew he was on the verge of topping himself. She got to the block of flats, grimly Soviet utility in their appearance and the lack of street lighting didn't help. She took the urinary lift to the fifth floor, found his door open and the man himself out on the balcony. 'Goodnight Bessie,' he had said, almost breezily, as he lifted one leg, then the other, over the railings. He hadn't died instantly. The hospital staff had enough time to transfuse every drop of blood in his mangled frame before he finally snuffed his candle.

Bessie'd seen the ad in her local paper. 'Ladies. Make extra money by telephone counselling. Feelgood factor high. Rewards considerable.' A plain brown envelope followed within days and the brochure inside sounded more like a part-time sociology degree than what it really was. There was also a cassette – various oddballs goofing off, the stories spawned by inadequacy and the age in which we live.

Bessie had to listen to a lot of weird stuff. In the early days she had to scribble down unfamiliar words on the kitchen planner, using a wash-off green felt pen. She learned about bitwins and straight twins. As she explained it to her friend Phyllis who popped round for a scone tea one afternoon 'a straight twin is where two women, usually prostitutes are hired for a ménage a trois and they concentrate their efforts on the bloke, but in the bi-twin they concentrate on each other and the bloke just watches.' Phyllis found her friend's new world engrossing, could see how Bessie was somehow charged up by it. A departure from the routine, although Bessie swore that, after a while, it became itself routine, the breathy conversations as mechanical as any. Sometimes Phyllis would excuse herself, 'I really must powder my nose' but once in the sanctuary of the bathroom she would scribble down more unfamiliar words – gay terms like 'watersports', 'brunch' and 'rimming' which she would look up in the library. None of the dictionaries shed any light.

Thankfully Bessie seldom had to say much herself. That's what made her agency different, from all those scripted, bimbette scripts, with their instructions to 'moan here'. All Bessie had to do, usually, was listen to these men getting off on themselves. Sometimes she wanted to tell one of the inveterate swearers to wash his mouth out with carbolic, but every call was worth at least a pound, and she'd learned the knack of listening with one ear closed, thumbing through a magazine. She could be reading about the latest antics of the Royal Family while some accountant got all lathered about piercing, or a regular, whose name was Sopwith, and a poet, judging from the colour of his metaphors, talked about surfing on pudenda or diving in deep. He was full of images of the sea, like Jung, or the shipping forecast. Sopwith phoned twice a week. Hadn't had sex for twenty three years.

Then, one Thursday morning, on a day too wet to hang out washing, there came a man's voice which resonated with something else. Not something cheap, or force-fed with a diet of skin-flicks and whacko magazines. This voice, clear and somehow honest, told of love.

'I'd like to read you a poem, if I may.'

And he read a short poem by Elizabeth Jennings about love and stars and it was so fine and wonderfully wrought – with that one perfect stanza 'The star's impulse/Must wait for eyes to claim it beautiful/And love arrived may find us somewhere else.' She wrote the whole thing down, word by word, with him paying for every one with his American Express card. She thanked him – itself the strangest departure – and she felt that his one call had undone, unsoured so many of the hours of sexual bleating and oddness.

She waited for another call, but for ten days there were only the dribbling masturbators, the peeping Toms, the material fetishists.

'Are you wearing rubber?' one would ask her and she wanted to tell him the truth, describe herself in the mirror, down to the Do-Ray-Me slippers and the nylon housecoat bought from the Kays catalogue.

'Yes, and I had to rub talcum powder all over my breasts just to get in it, it's so tight.'

That sort of thing would be enough to elicit a groan or three which would give her time to throw the switch on the kettle, or set a frond of fern into her ongoing floral decoration.

She was just having a real treat, Colombian coffee with evaporated milk in lieu of milk or cream, when the phone went. She'd almost decided to pack it in for the day, put on the Ansafone, but, hearing the ring, thought she could do with the money, especially as she was going on the WI trip to Hereford the following week.

'Is that you Rose?' Rose was Bessie's professional name.

'Yes it is.'

'It's Harry. I think I've fallen in love with your voice, for no other reason than that it's old beyond your years. You don't sound like a twenty three year old. You sound about fifty five, like a widow I once knew, with a small shadow of grief hidden behind all her words.'

Bessie felt as if she'd been rumbled, as if this voice, this man, had watched her from the cover of the shrubbery, unearthed her secret. She was exactly, exactly (!) fifty five, and her Scotty'd passed away eight years ago. She felt guilty thinking about him, about how he'd feel if he heard what came down the receiver sometimes. That kind man with his monster, winning smile. But if he'd paid his pension regularly none of this would have happened. She didn't do it out of choice. Well, not entirely. After the Samaritans she had missed her evening confessionals. It was like 'Book at Bedtime', only more gripping.

Harry phoned again on Thursday. This time he was clear.

'I want to meet you, Rose, if that's indeed your real name. I really want to meet you.'

Bessie's heart lurched back and fore in its cage. There were strict rules. And then a flash. The last time she'd gone to meet someone. His broken body splayed out among the lupins.

'I can't Harry. I simply can't.'

And that was it. The last phone call from a man who seemed to know the truth about her. Men like that didn't grow on trees.

She got a little down after that. A sadness crept in. Despite throwing herself into an orgy of jam making – perfecting her gooseberry and quince, mixing up the bucket of dewberries she'd picked on the local sand-dunes with tight, bitter little crabapples, straining a translucent greengage conserve which seemed to have trapped the sun itself within the jars, making a classic strawberry jam and some Seville marmalade, with thick pieces of rind, she still felt low as low can be. She consoled herself with the thought that the man, Harry, might have been clinical, there were all sorts out there. She'd spoken to a couple of thousand of them.

The following Tuesday she invited Phyllis round. Asked her if she'd like to take over the service, become a therapist like herself, with Bessie retaining a small cut, just to pay for her hobbies. Phyllis agreed with alacrity. She loved a good chat. Helped herself to another scone, just to celebrate.

Turning into Papa

One Thursday morning Clem Thomas of 33, Orchid View, Abersych, woke up and became Ernest Hemingway. If truth be told, he often did change identity – usually choosing to be someone more famous than himself which, being the invisible sort of unemployed vegetable-grader wasn't too difficult. At a recent party at the 'Slug and Lettuce' a girl had asked him, 'What do you do?' lurchingly gripping her pint. When he'd told her that he graded vegetables, sorting out the big carrots from the little ones, that sort of thing, she'd just walked away, without a word. Even before he could tell her about the funny shaped Brussels sprouts he'd found – the ones shaped like Martians and the ones with little arms.

His mother, Ettie, was sick to the back teeth with Clem's funny ways. Only last week he'd spent the day as Charlie Sheen in the film 'Apocalypse Now'. Every so often Clem would run in and yell 'Napalm attack! Everybody down!' expecting her to dive to the kitchen floor but she was, well, getting too old for that sort of thing, – she'd rather run the risk of napalm burns! But her only son had been doing this for years. When he was a kid he was forever dressing up – cowboy outfits, astronaut suits, the man from UNCLE, Manchester United football kit – you name it, he was in it. Once she had found him dressed up in her own clothes but he'd grown out of that one, bless the stars. Clem was never happier than when he wasn't being himself. It was his way of dealing with life on the skids.

Hemingway, he reckoned, would be easy. Clem had been the forty-first reader of 'The Life of Hemingway' in the borough library. All he'd need to do, he reckoned to himself while shaving, was indulge in a bit of heavy-duty drinking, that is if his giro stretched that far. He would act tough and play hard. He wouldn't bother with the writing bit though, that was poncy. He couldn't for the life of him understand why old Ernest had spent so much time in front of a big, clanking old machine of a typewriter when all the fun was to be had smoking, drinking, womanising and fishing.

Aye, fishing. Which was precisely why Clem was tucking his bus pass in his duffle coat pocket, and catching the number fifty two to Barry Docks.

The top deck looked as if a gas grenade had gone off. Clem counted them all – twenty two smokers hard at work trying to create enough of a fug to obscure the sign which read' Positively No Smoking. Maximum fine £100'. Underneath someone had added, 'If God hadn't meant us to smoke he wouldn't have given us lungs'. That sounded familiar.

In the misted window Clem caught a glimpse of a tall man, say six-foot-one, a Nobel prize-winning tough guy with a passion for bull fights. Then the condensation started running rivulets down the window pane, and Papa Hemingway dissolved away just as the bus passed the new leisure centre.

A solitary sandwich board in the public part of the docks announced that there was one sea-fishing trip leaving that morning, a noon sailing on the Azure Princess, which turned out to be a sleek if sea-worn craft with a small blue cabin and a captain called Boyle. Clem rubbed his hands together. So far so good. All right, the boats Hemingway had messed about in were longer, whiter, bigger, with chrome rails which were moored under a Florida sky, but this was a start. Hemingway would have certainly have approved of the skipper's face, a face with the sort of lived-in look that suggested a hell of a lot of people had been living in it, and throwing wild parties to boot. There were so many lines on it that the good Captain looked like a geological feature or maybe one of those people they'd fished out of a peat bog, crazily preserved.

He yelled down to the good captain.

'What are you going after, Captain?'

'Anything you like, pal, seeing as you're the only punter wanting to take to the high seas this morning. Whaddya fancy?

'I dunno. Marlin maybe. Tarpon, or maybe beach up in a river mouth and try for snook. Get any of those around here?'

The captain looked perplexed.

'We're the wrong side of the ocean, my friend. The only sure fire certainty around here this time of year is mackerel, probably conger out on the wrecks and a possibility of cod. Not on drugs are you?'

'No, I've just been reading a lot of Hemingway recently.'

'What, the muscular prose stylist?'

'Aye. The same sniff. Can I book up for the twelve o'clock voyage Captain?'

'We can leave right away. I am intrigued.'

Clem lifted his French Army duffle bag over the handrail. The bottle of Jack Daniel's bourbon, and the sandwiches his mother had cut for him were safely inside.

The sea beyond the harbour mouth was pewter and unruffled. Mind you, Clem had a twinge of regret that he hadn't taken his mum's offer of a couple of 'Quells'. Clem's sea-legs were made of Rowntrees' jelly.

The engine spluttered into life and the small craft wore a cloak of diesel as it cu-cu-coughed its way down mid-channel past the green and red harbour lights. After half an hour of full steam ahead the boat chugged to a coasting halt. Captain Boyle produced a bucket of mackerel from, hell what was it called, you know, downstairs on a ship? They began to prepare the bait – Captain Boyle's knife looking sharp enough to cut itself – and started threading the fish onto some line. He felt it a pity to violate these beautiful fish with their grey tiger stripes and shirt-button eyes, but after a few minutes the bucket of bait was ready.

The Captain lit a roll-your-own cigarette.

'There are a couple of tidy wrecks under us here: like Butlins they are for conger eels which are as big as a man's arm some of them, as big as yourself Mr Hemingway, or may I call you Ernest?'

'Call me Papa. All my friends do.'

'Sure thing Papa.'

The chunks of mackerel went down with their lead and Clem cracked open the bottle of sour-mash whisky. He wondered how well it would go with chopped pork and Branston pickle sarnies. The sun shafted through a gap in the clouds and Clem felt warm enough to take off his shirt to reveal a T-shirt showing a perched scarlet macaw and the words 'Havana. El Ciudad Majico.' The magic city. Papa Hemingway had spent a lot of time there. Clem had looked up Cuba on the map. It was a long way away but Clem could reach it in his dreams. Like now. He felt the sun's warmth on his unfortunate tattoo which read 'Rhyl '87'. He gripped the handrail, pulled the ozone-charged air deep into his lungs. He felt as if he could take on the world, and spit out the pips.

Clem found himself telling Boyle about the funniest thing he's heard concerning the sea which had to with his Uncle Wilber who worked in the States, as a composer for films. One summer, Wilber's mother, Ethel, went out to visit him but, unfortunately, while in Los Angeles she passed away. Wilber had to have her body taken to one of the ports on the Eastern seaboard and shipped backed to Glanymwswl. When the cask arrived in the village they looked inside and found it wasn't Wilber's mother, but an admiral bedecked in medals. Wilber's mother had been buried at sea, with full naval honours!

Captain Boyle laughed so mightily he had to hold onto to Clem to stop himself falling over board and a bond was formed. It was true, see. Hemingway had always been a magnet for friends.

The first fish clamped on down in the green depths giving an almost imperceptible pull on the line. Then began the long haul, craggy Captain Boyle giving instructions in a voice so low and slow it seemed as if he was helping to seduce the fish out of its sea-bed. Suddenly Clem felt the whole weight and the lashing power of the fish as it came within reach. His arms bent like pipe cleaners.

'There she is,' hollered Boyle. 'It's a conger all right, sinuous and all muscle, built like a power lifter, and all yours. Haul it in amigo.'

And Clem did just that, pulling in the big eel with a perfect satisfaction. He handed it to Boyle to do the unpleasant business – the bang on the head. When the fish had been dispatched Clem paused to admire the serried ranks of needle-teeth, and lit a Marlboro with his all-weather Zippo lighter. The nicotine gave him a feeling of contentment, smugness even, then he started coughing with gusto. Clem didn't smoke normally, but Hemingway did, like his life depended on it.

Clem bathed in the sunshine and in the glory reflected off the big eel's body. Suddenly a central Asian dialect broke through on the ship's radio. Clem couldn't understand a word of it so he shouted to the Captain, now master of the bridge.

'Duw the reception's good on this set of yours. Picking up Mongolia are we?'

'No need to be sarcastic. It's Munny Jenkins, with the coastguard, all the way from Nash Point. It seems as if all the calm is about to go out of our lives.'

'Why what's up?' said Clem, remembering with anguished regret the packet of Quells on the dresser in the house.

'Looks like there's the mother of all storms blowing in,' and they both looked out towards the thin charcoal line of the horizon where, indeed, inky clouds were swirling in, looking angry and moving fast.

'This one's the tail end of a hurricane, apparently. They say it was so strong in the Caribbean that it's been raining coconut trees over Ireland on the way and a tanker captain swears he saw a bamboo cabin flying over the sea, heading for Galway.'

'You don't say.'

'I do say.'

'So, what are we going to do Captain?'

'Batten down the hatches and say a little prayer. It'll be on us any minute now.'

And it did whip up, fast, the waves becoming twisting sheets, and Clem lost his duffle bag and his breakfast of Ready Brek went over the side with the captain laughing like a maniac as he spun the ship's wheel first this way and that and the boat rocking back and forth like a flight simulator replicating a crash landing.

Clem imagined the swirling waters below as a great soup of mermaids, dolphins, huge wracks of frenzied seaweed and sea urchins, lots and lots of sea urchins. And he had paid seven quid for this – seven quid to go on a nightmare journey round the back of hell and beyond. He must be mad – clean off. Two Scotch eggs short of a picnic.

The boat seemed to have lost all weight, all gravity as it was tossed like a piece of balsa wood back and fore as if the waves had hands. A good clean hit of adrenaline sped through Clem's body but he calmed himself by imagining how Hemingway would have planted his big feet – well, Clem imagined he must have had big feet – planted them firmly on the deck and laughed into the eye of the storm, bellowing like one of his favourite Spanish bulls. But the waves grew bigger, bigger than houses, bigger than a block of flats and Clem suddenly saw himself, a small man being washed away into the oblivion of a big, angry sea. The sea-spray was fine and choking and Clem could only just make out the shape of Captain Boyle who seemed to be making something in the cabin. Clem wished it was a liferaft. Gripping the handrail for life itself Clem took a few faltering, terrified steps towards the cabin door. Boyle was tying himself to the wheel with a length of rope. That was rich. That was very rich. Clem thought, 'What about his paying, his Nobel prize winning passengers?' For the first time in his short life Clem felt a surge of anger welling up inside him and he went in the cabin door.

'Saving your own skin, pal.'

'Get out ya landlubber.'

That, unfortunately, was it – the trigger word. No-one had

ever called Clem a landlubber before – which was hardly surprising seeing as he lived in the middle of a council estate and only saw the sea during occasional holidays. Clem's fist tightened, his muscles tensed and then like a war-hardened Hemingway figure he slammed his fist against the side of the captain's head. It felt as if he'd hit a wall. The captain caught Clem's skull in a vice and seemed to start turning some ratchet or other slowly, causing exquisite state-of-the-art pains to shoot through. Then, behind the captain's bum he saw something red, something moving.

Munny Jenkins had sent the lifeboat which saved Clem from a good hiding if not saved his life. 'Lifeboat,' he grunted chokingly, as he twisted his neck to look at the captain, recognising the slightly glaze-eyed expression of a man who had, like himself, stared death in the face.

Clem Hemingway looked like a whipped dog when they finally steered in between the stone arcs of the harbour mouth. He was wet, weary and his conger was missing. In the litter bin on the bus stop he found a Sunday magazine which gave him a good idea. There was a big colour picture of Andre Previn. Tomorrow he would go into town and get himself a baton.

Sticca

The woodlands were silent, as if someone had smart-bombed the woodcutters. Or was it neutron bombed? No thunk of wedges driven into the soon-to-be-felled, no hornet whine of chainsaws, no clink of climbing irons, just the sussuration of wind through the sitkas. Even the tiny goldcrests were silent, the little sewing machines of their high-top voices seemingly out of juice. In a clearing, lush with bracken, some new born deer shivered with the fear of their first days, their camouflage perfect for cowering in the dappled breaks, but even with their bodies quivering they made no sound.

It confused the hell out of Billy Rowan, who had just arrived home after a week helping his uncle in a neighbouring forest with the fungus harvest. They filled big osier baskets with wood blewits, all pale violet flesh and gathered mounds of milk mushrooms, which grew in such profusion that they turned the forest glades into flows of buttermilk.

Billy was confused. He often maintained that life in the forest was far more confusing than any city. There was more data bombardment. More going on. More hazards, certainly. Tell that to any city dweller, reared on fear of muggers when they confront their first pack of wolves, smart and as shadowy as night itself. Those lemon yellow eyes, those meat-tearing teeth.

Confusing? Wandering through the people-less wood Billy thought life in the forest was a word salad. Super sitkas. Selective thinning. Dutch elm beetle. Blanket plantation. Sustainable harvests. Barbeque charcoal burners. Forest design plans. Tactical strike coppicing.

It was madder than, well, say São Paolo. More industrious

even, especially when the felling was in full swing. But not today. He walked down the 'G' path to the stream, following the secret trail system where the signals were notched into the lowermost branch of each turning-point-tree. Billy headed north-west towards the huts.

It was in Woodcutter Hut Four, set apart from the rest, that Billy'd had his first real confirmation that the century had caught up with the woodfolk.

One night he'd stumbled home from a rowanberry vodka tasting and noticed a strange, green glow coming out of the windows of the hut. Billy crept towards the glow on all fours, then peered in, only to see the stranger who had recently bought the hut sitting at the controls of what might have been a space ship. The strong liquor – newly concocted on Timmy Chestnut's best still – gave Billy the temerity to knock on the door and ask about the machine.

It transpired it was an electron microscope. It took pictures of the very smallest things, which the man then sold to scientific journals. All this in the dank green bowels of woods 'where life has remained unchanged for five centuries or more,' according to the Wildwood Tourism Bureau's latest brochure.

There was talk of new visitor apartments being built on the holly groves, planted by his great great grandfather. The men in suits who arrived on the edge of the woods in their gleaming cars had no idea what they were doing.

Billy knew hollywood to be a hard, fine, white-grained wood, the tree well able to cope with cold, the waxy leaves stopping water loss when the ground is frozen to iron underfoot and likewise able to grow even after fire has blackened it, or burnt it to a stump. The crown of thorn spines and the blood of Christ berries. Sacred.

They would cut down the grove simply so that goggle-eyed city folk could come and peer into their huts and flashgun in their faces. No way. Over his dead one.

There was the distant bee rumble of conversation at the top of the ride. It seemed as if all the woodfolk had convened for some reason or other. Billy hoped it was the threat to the holly grove but as he arrived Harry Lime was clearing his throat to address the crowd.

'The Stick Chooser, Teddy Beech is dying. There has never been a time when knowing the old ways was more important, you might say, imperative. Who's game and brave?'

Not one hand went up. Whilst many men knew the truth of what he said they also knew they'd have to suffer to prove themselves worthy of the knowledge. It was as if they all had a collective phobia about snakes.

Billy was scared – no doubt about that – but with a trembling deep within his muscles he raised a hand.

'I'll do it,' he said, looking at the crowd which was all crazy angles as people craned forward to look.

'Fetch the adders then,' said Lime, his voice raven-croaky with expectation.

The hessian sacks pulsed and shifted with the movements of the trapped serpents. Billy stripped to the waist and thought of techniques he'd read about in a dentist's waiting room for dealing with stress. He breathed in deep, the air coursing down the estuarine channels of his lungs. He thought of comforting thoughts – cotton wool clouds and soft labrador puppies. But they didn't halt the adrenaline rush, the bio-shock that had every nerve ending on red alert, that helped him put his hand in the sack.

There was only one blackadder among the writhing coils of ordinary adders. As old Harry said, 'All you have to do is find the right viper with your hands and bring it out into the light. They say the shape of its head is different but I don't know . . . '

The snakes were angry, having been lifted out of the comfort of their pit with its plentiful rat chicks and ignominiously dumped in the sack. Their forked tongues flickered with delight as they sensed the vibration of a tremulous set of fingers coming through the dark toward them. Billy wished he'd been able to drop some phenobarbitone tablets, or at the very least a Librium 5, but he'd not had time to visit the bird cherries where he kept his stash of drugs.

He could feel his fingers dropping pearls of sweat as he palped around in the sack. How could he tell colour in the dark? Was the black one bigger? Meaner?

He knew the snake had been handled at least once before, when the Stick Chooser had himself inherited the mantle. The snakes were warm, like the fermented insides of a haystack, a foetid bundle of tails and sightless eyes and hypodermic fangs loaded with enough toxins to still a rat's heart with one pumping drop.

Billy felt a tingle in the tip of his index digit as he stroked the head of a snake, his fingers closing around its throat and tugging it free from the twisted mass of other snakes.

The excited exhalations of the crowd turned to cheering within seconds. They offered him a jeroboam of elderflower champagne which he shook like a Formula One racing car driver before showering it over their exulting heads.

In the middle of the celebrations he felt an insistent tug at the hem of his jacket. It was Harry Lime.

'Time to go.'

The old, dying man sounded as if he had a chest full of budgerigars as he struggled for breath, the fine pipes of his lungs blocked by age and sickness. This was Terry Beech, the Stick Chooser, the nearest thing they had to a shaman.

A couple of years previously an anthropologist from Berkeley, California had written a thesis about him. Even the most learned of the woodlanders couldn't understand it when the fat volume arrived. It was all a jumble of mathematical figures and words that weren't in the dictionary.

The American lady had failed to get the point. The point was this. The stick was the ultimate symbol of knowing the woods, it proclaimed allegiance to it, an at-one-ness with it, a semiotic shorthand for 'This man is a woodlander who understands the way trees grow and has himself grown in tandem with them and now that he is gnarled himself he is ready to rest under their shading canopy.'

Mr Beech's eyes were rheumy with age and watery with pain. His lungs' broken windbag of an accordion made up a tortured melody.

'Did the snake speak to you?' asked Beech, each word a bird breaking free.

'It spoke through touch,' said Billy.

'Ah!' said the old man, in a tone which suggested that this was the right answer.

'So listen . . . '

And so the Stick-Chooser shared his wisdom with Billy, who displayed an accipitrine attentiveness, hanging on his every word.

Beech told him to 'Pick the stick in winter, when the sap is low, so the bark won't shrink. Oak is good, ash is good, cherry's good but the ash is full of knots. Ashes without blemish grow in sheltered places. Look for hazel where the trees are many and the twigs grow from the sides most desperate for the light. The best handle for the hazel is the root, so cut down as well as up. Leave the wood rest for a year before shaping.'

The old man mouthed wordlessly like a goldfish as he searched the corners of his brain for more to say. His brain was desiccated by age. Should some kind fellow stave in his skull he would surely find the sort of dust you find when you crack open a very old walnut. He was sure of it.

'Store the wood in sacking. Shape it as a taper for tapers make for balance. The balance is found at a spot one third of the length from the handle The handle must be at a right angle to the walker so his weight falls directly on it.'

By now Billy didn't think he had to concentrate too hard on what the old man was saying. It was as if he knew it deep within – blackthorn is pliable and alder works when wet – was a part of the information handed on with his father's genes.

The old man pointed an arthritic finger, as gnarled as the worst ever specimen of knotted ash, at the oak stick in the corner.

'Let that be your template.' And with that he died, with a soft sound like a bat fluttering by.

Billy had already had his eye on the precise tree which would yield the stick, a symbolic staff of a thing which had the limitlessness of growth about it. He cut it the next day, though wildly out of season. It needed to be a heavy stick, ready for hard use. He coloured the end of it with a few drops of robin blood, sacrificed in the old way, its tiny heart still bleeding. He gave it a name – Sticca – a name his matted-haired ancestors would recognise.

When the stick was ready Billy set out for the city. He took Wildtrail 14 down to the sumach grove, then took a straight route along Plainway 41.

Two days later he arrived at the offices of the developers who were set to move their earthmoving monsters into the sacred groves of his beloved forest. Paying no attention to the prize-heavyweight security guards, Billy marched to the second floor with its boardroom, art works and banks of computers. Sticca, wielded with a ferocity of a spirit that pulsed through Billy with the screaming violence of a polecat crunching down a leveret, smashed its way through the offices, with women screaming and porcelain art works bought from masters in Kyoto turned into so much shrapnel.

By the time the police arrived in sufficient numbers to arrest him – and only then with the use of a stun gun – Billy had managed to set the mainframe computer on fire and throw a water cooler through the smoked glass table around which the obese toad directors sat in terrified puffiness.

The policeman who interrogated Billy said they could only begin to help him if he handed them the stick. He had held on to it as if it was welded to his fingers with Araldite. A burly Special Branch officer had tried to prise it from Billy's hand with a screwdriver but even that had failed. Billy stared sullenly at the goon who grew so angry that he began to exude a faint red halo of light, which drifted into the corners of the room and served to make him look demonic.

Grown tired of Billy's insolence, the man motioned to the

goons behind the two-way mirror, unlovable as hepatitis. They stormed in and four weightlifter-types pinned Billy's arms to the floor.

'It's only a stick for Chrissake,' said the officer, his face swollen with triumph into the shape of a distorted balloon. The stick was tossed to him and he twirled it like a majorette's baton.

'It's the spirit of the place, the soul of the woods,' said Billy plaintively, tears welling, his anguish hot knives in the flesh.

The goons roared, their laughter septic with spite.

'If you damage the stick the forest will weep,' said Billy, incanting and repeating the words so that they were delivered as a mantra.

'The forest will weep . . . '

' . . . Will weep.'

The interrogating policeman narrowed his eyes to slits and snapped the stick in two over his knee.

Billy crumpled to the floor.

In the forest a leaf fell from a tree and then another. Tens of leaves turned into hundreds and then thousands, great drifts of green leaves from wild service trees and hawthorns, cockspur thorns and tremulous aspens. Sour cherries became skeletons and larches lost their cover as all the trees became denuded, as autumn came suddenly in July. Soon this green would be a desert-land, parched and naked as any stretch of the Sahara.

'Do you see what you've done?' sobbed Billy, staring at the policeman who wore his mask of stupidity with the sort of pride that sometimes leads to genocide.

'See what you've done?'

In the forest, in that silence, a leaf snapped tinily from its stem-hold and began the last fall.

Amputation Wednesday

I'd written some tough guy lines for Hector Rosario to use when he was putting the squeeze on one of the Russians who had muscled in on his patch. Hector had gone along to the Russian's house with the script nearly word perfect, carrying the usual big pickling jar full of snakes which is one of his hallmarks. However, one of my sentences had the wrong effect. Now Hector said he's 'going to pull my lungs out of my throat' which is pretty ironic seeing as that's a phrase I gave him in a hundred dollar script only last year. The miserable miscreant.

Apparently it had all started swimmingly, with the Implied Threat Speech going down like tinned peaches:

'Listen you whorebag, you better groove on out of my slice of town or you can start buying your painkillers maxipack. Comprende, ya bag of spent fuck?'

I liked the poetic width of the last phrase – meaningless and meaning-laden at one and the same time – though it was probably wasted on the Russian who was probably better blessed with chunky gold jewellery from Turkmenistan than a grasp of grammar.

The rattlesnake Hector held up to his eyeball would have forced him to appreciate the scansion of the sentence. Unfortunately, my next line about his father being a gimp blue-touch-papered a supernova of anger in the man. His father actually was a paraplegic, a victim of a runaway piece of machinery in Donetsk. How was I to know? The Russian Mafioso snatched the snake from Hector's hand. He crushed its skull between his thumb and forefinger so that grey matter and blood spilled like jam out of a doughnut on either side.

Words are more powerful than swords, than a rattlesnake's lunge, than a magnum held against one's temple. It is the words 'Tell me where the money is or I'll scatter your intelligence across the living room' that gets you squealing, all supergrass-bleating, rather than the cold rim of loaded metal against your head. Metonymy always works – 'intelligence' equals 'brains' is ideal stuff when putting on the frighteners. In twenty years of scripting for thugs – it's like being a writer in Hollywood except the hoods are real, the blood ain't ketchup and the actors take a little longer to learn their lines – I've found that a little ambivalence can make a victim wither with fear. Words can bring out the tang in the violence.

Not that any of this gets me out of the deep trough of despair. Thanks to truth mirroring art in the shape of a one-armed, one-legged thoroughgoingly paraplegic Russian mining engineer, here I am trying to find the lie in the words 'No Hiding Place'. This is Anonymity Central, sleeping with down-and-out panhandlers in a room which smells of fungicide mixed with toxic-dump-style rancid sweat. My bunk bed companion, Gainly, is a born-again Christian whose wife left him for his son and he has dealt with that Oedipal pisser by drinking furniture polish and paint-stripper cocktails washed down with bilious bitterness. He says he knows I am an educated man – he can tell from the way I say 'No thank you' when he offers me a swig.

The note I got from Hector frightened me to the marrow. It was made up of letters cut from newspapers, what I call terrorist-typeface.

Dear Vic,
I am going to amputate you on Wednesday. Cold-heartfelt wishes, Hector.
That's a perfect example of the same sort of simplicity at work as the graffito on the New York Subway – the one that says 'You,' where you're left to fill in the rest of the threat to your person, if threat it is. Hector's was a line that held you like dental pliers. Which Wednesday? Amputate what

precisely? I had my doubts about his surgical standards – replacement prosthetics was not, perhaps, a consideration.

Nursing a tin cup of Gainly's home-made, gut-rot wine – made without loving care from discarded teabags – I pondered my predicament. Most every option was closed to me. I was running through a town of cul-de-sacs – the bloodhounds freshly unleashed from their transportation lorries, the soundtrack to the day the sound of knives on whetstones stropping to sharpness.

I'm not what you'd call a violent man: in fact, try craven coward, The Man With The Jellyfish Spine. But I wasn't going to let it show in the letter I was penning. I wasn't going to give up my tongue or whatever without some show of defiance.

Dear Hector, (that's right, appeal to that hint of a vestige of friendship that crept into our business transactions – don't give him cause to short fuse yet.) Thank you for your note. I was sorry to hear about the problems with Mr Urna and my condolences over the death of Spitter. He was a brave snake. I am, of course, concerned about the amputation scenario. Perhaps there is some way we could work this out amicably? Yours in supplication,
Vic.

Defiant, huh?

I hand delivered the letter to a drinking clinic Hector frequents, having made ridiculously complicated arrangements for collecting the returning message – a convoluted chain of contacts and drops including a key exchange at my aunt's house. Aunt Betty's amnesiac – so even if Hector should trace the line that far and tried his Syrian interrogation routine on her – she'd have nothing much to tell, only the usual addled nonsense which goes 'Weather's brightening . . . weather's brightening . . .' Betty's needle stuck forever in the groove. Even Hector with his extra chromosome should realise she's not worth warming the electrodes for.

The message came back quicker than I thought, so fast that I thought for an instant that he might have found himself another scriptwriter. A good one at that – minimal, a master of concision. No greeting, no sign-off. We'll make the amputation amicable. Next Wednesday convenient? Name your body part. Love to Gainly.

So, I'd been followed all the way back to my snoring companion. Hector was seriously going to lop off a part of me. As it happened next Wednesday wasn't convenient as I'd been forced to have an interview with a social worker, but let's face it no Wednesday in all my remaining days would be convenient for a spot of limb stripping. The walls of the hostel were dripping blood, agglutinous and molasses-black. It was clear that I was going to have to write the letter of my life.

This was no time to be having writer's block but when I pulled my writing kit out of the all-I-have-in-the-whole-wide-world haversack and set them on the desk in the security guard's Portakabin in the grounds of the doss-house I realised that the English language simply hasn't got the words, even in quite glorious permutation, to disable all my demons. The pad of yellow legal paper and the Watermans' pen mocked me.

I went for a walk along the embankment, tried word assocation, then a spot of paronomasia – a spot of idle punning – anything to get a sentence going but all I could conjure up was a visual image – myself swimming nakedly in the deep end of a David Hockney style swimming pool as burly men emptied huge metal vats of unspeakable material into the water – dog heads, turds, rotting veg and hospital waste. Doing the backstroke was no way out.

The missive to save my life had to avoid sycophancy. Hector knew an arselicker at a thousand paces. With an angel perched precariously on my shoulder, I kick started the letter.

Dear Hector,
I know you to be a gambling man. I'll wager a part of my body on a game of Scrabble. Find your challenger and I'll

take him or her on. If I win I stay in one piece: if I lose you take away a piece. Hope this sounds fair. Wednesday would be fine.
Yours sincerely,
Vic.

I hoped he appreciated that ironic touch about the Wednesday. I took the letter down to Marciano's Casino. The doorman said he'd been expecting me, which sent a liquid nitrogen shiver down my spine.

I really believed that Hector would go for it. He had the gambling gene, sure as eggs is eggs. And I was confident about the game. I knew the Greek alphabet by heart, which is all there in Chambers' dictionary. I could slot the word 'adze' into one of the corners, making for a redoubtable score.

Wednesday was a misty day with an underwater sun struggling to rise to the surface of the canal. As I walked along the towpath I rehearsed some of my best Scrabble lists. Such as all the words including a 'q' not followed by a 'u' – 'buqsha', 'faqir', 'qaid', 'suq', 'umiaq', 'tranq', – all sing-songing through my brain like a mantra.

I went and bought a suit, rehearsing favourite words as I ran my fingers through the racks, laying them onto ghost Scrabble grids – 'petrace', 'misenroll', and double 'v' words like 'slivovics', along with old faves like 'thermits', 'declaws', you know, all the dizzying cornucopia.

There was just one problem. I'd been beaten every time I'd played. Seldom by too many points and always against good players, but my pedigree didn't include a deal of winning.

It was seven thirty precisely when I arrived at the room of my destiny. The fact that Fabbrizio Montale, the thug on the door, was loading up on crack cocaine didn't augur well. Inside there was a thick fug of marijuana smoke, a purple haze in which people seemed to grope their way around the room. It seemed like too much the party. But as my eyes accustomed to the gloom they alighted on a beheading block set in the middle of a boxing ring, surrounded by tiers of seating filled already by some of the seriously psychotic and preposterously wealthy crims in the city.

There was Jimmy Jimenez, a cocaine baron of such wealth that when he was caught in a huge operation sanctioned by George Bush himself which included helicopter gunships swooping down on Jimmy's villa he offered to buy his freedom by paying off Bolivia's external debt. This man was richer than a good many countries, which was bad news for me because the side bets would be measurable in terms of Burkina Fasso's gross national product.

Hector was slipping hundred dollar bills into the cleavage of one of the Armenian lapdancers. He nodded at me just as one of his meatsack henchmen came over to his table, which stood in front of the man with the scimitar. A scimitar for Chrissake! How can a man work miracles on the Scrabble table when he's got – Jesus, I recognised him – when he's got Razor fucking Eddie at the controls of a scimitar that looks like it could shave samples fit to place under a microscope? I caught his eye, a bad move because I got a glimpse of how a rabbit feels when mesmerised by a weasel. Eddie can look at you as if he's just about to ingest your brains through a straw.

The killer question now as who was my opponent, but I didn't have to wait on that one. A gawky spotty youth in backwards-facing baseball cap and combat trousers was escorted to his chair. A minor-league movie actor whose name I couldn't recall took hold of a microphone and made an announcement:

'Gentlemen, the bout is about to begin. You all know Vic Hazlemere, writer and raconteur and it gives me greater pleasure to introduce Waverley Kennedy, current reigning Scrabble champion of New York State . . . '

The applause was shocking as firecrackers. It crackled around the room even as I took a sharp intake of breath –

61

relieved beyond measure that that this wasn't the all American champion Scrabble player seated in front of me, and as the compere announced . . .

' . . . and reigning champion of all the rest of this great country of ours.'

Waverley looked startled, a deer trapped in the headlights of a hurtling Mac truck.

I won the toss of the coin and took no time at all to slam down 'sjambok' – 'to flog' in Malay, hoping that I could unsettle the nerd with just this opening gambit. His reply, delivered with confident clicks of the letters on the board, was a word I'd never heard of. I had to weigh up the pros and cons of challenging it and showing a vulnerable ignorance or brazening it out. I looked at my rack of letters, shuffling them around looking for a way to get rid of all seven letters but the best I could manage was four and that was with a word which set off every fucker in the room laughing because the word was 'sword' at which cue Eddie with a demonic grin lifted the scimitar a few inches above the block. I felt my testicles lift and disappear into my body cavity with fear.

Waverley, his movements robotic, splayed out a weedy hand and put down the word 'thermit'.

'That's one of my words' I thought even as I realised that my opponent had probably absorbed, had bloody well learned the Webster dictionaries on both sides of the Atlantic by rote and that Eddie wasn't going to be disappointed in his need for a blood-letting.

Out of the corner of my eye I saw fat bundles of money changing hands.

I pulled back a few points with my next three of four words and I managed to get in the word 'umiaq' which seemed to phase Boy Wonder.

Then I had to miss a go, at which a sigh went round the room and lifted like a banshee through an open window. Weeeow!

Then Waverley delivered a killer blow, triple word, triple letter, double fucking z. 'Lezzes.' What on God's earth were they? When I appealed a triumphant Hector brought me the dictionary on a silver drinks' tray and offered me a magnifying glass so I could see the word better.

Trailing hopelessly I could feel my guts slide with terror. I only had four pieces left on the rack. A.R.D. But then it came to me and the space was there and I put them all in place, not enough to win the game but enough to constitute a last and desperate psychological gambit. An acronym. 'Dora,' from the Defence of the Realm Act, 1914. And the name of Hector's five year old daughter. He couldn't sanction a slaughter in the shadow of her blessed name could he?

The room held its breath, faces turning towards the man. Then Hector laughed a huge laugh – ripe as exploding fruit, a great stentorian bellow.

'You win, Vic,' he said, 'you win,' doubling up now, chortling fit to burst.

His words were euphonious and I thought of a glass harmonica, the euphon someone had made in the eighteenth century. My testicles started their downward journey. Jimmy Jimenez gave me a tequila slammer along with a share of his winnings. He knew I'd come up trumps. The villains were all smiling like this was Boys' Club and they'd just been watching a fly-tying demonstration.

Waverley shook my hands and I felt a smile of extravagant relief spreading from ear to ear. The strong spirits kept the smile wide, the bubbles from the soda rising up to the occipital bone of my skull.

And then I thought, 'What's in a word, eh?'

The Frost Hollow

The Frost Hollow is just a small bowl in the dank earth of the woods, beyond the stands of silver birch and the tangles of withered brambles. In the middle of the hollow a pond is locked into place throughout the winter because the hollow is beyond the reach of the thin arms of sunlight which break through the treetops. It is a home for the chill wind.

Beyond the woods which fringe the hollow stands the clapperboard house, its primrose walls peeling now, now that the parents are gone, leaving grandmother to look after the two children. There is David, aged nine and his sister, Florence who's a year older. She calls him Carrothead because of his rusty orange hair and he, being the politest sort of nine year old, calls his sister Florence because that is her name. David wouldn't dream of using nicknames.

And then there is Grandmother Mabel, whose age has more numbers in it than a long division sum. She is old enough to be ancient.

The house has a big porch where, on summer evenings, grandmother knits stories for the two of them, her needles keeping time. 'Clickety, clackety, click.' She tells them her own tales, tales of the family and stories about places far away. 'Click, click, click.'

One July evening – when the scent of flowers in the garden was as powerful as opening a bottle of perfume – Grandmother Mabel recited a story which seemed as if it might never end. She called it 'War and Peace' and said that her mother taught it to her when she was growing up. Grandmother remembers lots of things.

Florence and David live with their grandmother because, one day the parents had had an argument, each threatening to leave. They were so furious that they trailed great streamers of dark blue steam behind them. The parents strode across the fields, one heading east, one heading west and never looked back.

Grandmother Mabel sometimes tells them stories about the mother and father, the words so vivid that they can sometimes hear the mother moving baking trays in the kitchen and smell the sour new dough, or hear the thunk of the father's axe outside at the woodpile.

The house was very silent after their mother and father had gone. It was so silent that you could hear a moth's wings as it came in close to the light. So quiet that you could not only hear a pin drop but the sound of it dropping would have been enough to make the cats jump in the air, almost leaving their skins behind. The striking of the grandfather clock sounded like a thunderstorm breaking in the hall before the house wrapped itself in its quilt of silence once again.

The children didn't play any more. David didn't say a word for three whole weeks. Florence walked around and around her room, mile after mile, until the day Grandmother Mabel came in and started measuring the room with a reel of tape. Grandmother scratched her head a few times before putting some numbers in pencil on a piece of card.

'You've already walked to Swansea and back,' said Grandmother Mabel who had worked out how far Florence had walked without getting anywhere.

'I think it's about time we made a little noise around here,' said the old lady, with purpose in her voice.

Grandmother Mabel had made great preparations. The children stared at her from the upstairs landing as she paraded around the hallway with a big drum hanging around her neck which she beat with a furious rhythm. She juggled strings which were attached to tin cans which had been converted into little bells and blew with all her might into a blue plastic trumpet which David recognised as one he used to play with years ago.

'And that's just the fanfare. Watch this!' Grandmother Mabel disappeared out the front door and the children had to move into the front bedroom to watch her. She was putting on a pair of enormous plastic ear-muffs and was applying a lighted match to a piece of string which hung from an old bucket which seemed to be full of dark soil.

'Tee, hee!' Grandmother Mabel tittered, exactly like a cartoon grandmother. 'Stand well back,' she shouted as she ran behind the hedge, her excited eyes peering out from behind the privet. Then, an ALMIGHTY explosion blew up the bucket and startled some nearby rooks so much that the birds flew away and kept on flying until they reached Finland. Grandmother Mabel had used an awful lot of gunpowder.

She heard the children laughing in the house and it was the happiest sound she'd ever heard. She now knew she could fill the emptiness in their lives.

Grandmother Mabel came inside and David and Florence were still laughing, due mainly to the fact that grandmother hadn't actually stood sufficiently well back and her face was covered in soot as if she'd just squeezed down the chimney. What with her white hair and the streaks of black all over face Grandmother Mabel looked like a skunk.

'Shall we have a tea party,' asked Grandmother as she wiped her face in a towel.

'Yes, let's,' came the little chorus. The children raced into the kitchen where the treats were already laid out. Greengage jam. Drop scones. Thin strips of brown bread and butter. After the children had gorged themselves, Grandmother Mabel told them some more stories and then they went to bed to sleep the sleep of the contented.

The ancient Greeks believed that after summer swallows slept at the bottom of ponds. The children believed it too and talked about it as they carried their home-made skates made of pummelled tin cans and balsa wood down to the hollow on a dark December day.

The Hollow was sighing softly as they trod gingerly around

the rim of the ice. They heard the crisp bark of the ice as it shored up the weight of them above, sharp as a fox-cry.

Under the grey surface of the pool David spotted something like frogspawn.

'They are eyes,' said Florence, 'the eyes of swallows – the last ones of the year. They must have been flying overhead when the pond froze over and it caught their reflections.'

A little confused, David sat on an alderstump and strapped on his skates. The winter sun was low over the fields as the two children got up a head of steam, racing in tight zig-zags and skidding wildly. The sprays of ice-splinters that flew behind them as they U-turned and careered round created miniature and instant rainbows. The splinters flew up into the air, taking shape, bright and fast, like tiny swallows taking wing.

Grandmother had roasted chestnuts for their return. She'd also made some cherryade with heaps of brown sugar.

The old lady had spent the afternoon watching waxwings in the garden. These were bright, showy birds which had come all the way from Russia to gorge on the berries of her cotoneaster bush. She had counted one bird eat three hundred and sixty berries, twice its own weight, before being dislodged from its perch in a hurry by the children hoot-footing it across the yard. Grandmother Mabel was surprised the greedy bird could fly at all, carrying all those red berries inside its straining stomach. But then again it was a long flight over the North Sea for a bird no bigger than her hand. It must have been very hungry after coming all that way.

'We saw swallows grandmother,' said the children as they took off their muddy boots in the hallway.

Not to be outdone Grandmother Mabel announced, 'I saw waxwings, children' and she told them all about the taiga – the frozen wastelands of the north, a cold expanse in Scandinavia and the freezing rim of Russia, where the berry crop had that year failed, the wastelands where probably the hollow had its ancestors. Florence and David's faces were mirrors held up to her marvels: the cherryade was voted number one drink of all time.

The children didn't go to school like other children. They didn't need to. Grandmother knew it all – not that she was a know all – she just knew it all. She helped them paint all the countries of the world around the walls of the landing and as they painted she told them One Important Fact.

When they painted Iceland she told them how the hardness of ice is similar to concrete. When they painted Canada she explained how the pines around the vast lakes grow so densely that the snow stays on top of the trees so the ground stays bare. She told them the Dead Sea has so much salt in it that people float on the surface and it is almost impossible to drown. And having painted a sun above and seven seas around two hundred and fifty two countries they drew the house with the three of them on the porch and the two cats – one on the roof and the other trotting across the fields after a day's hard mousing – and in letters tall as the sky they wrote the letters 'H.O.M.E.'

After they'd put the paint away and washed the brushes clean Grandmother Mabel gave them hot cocoa which they were allowed, as a treat, to drink in bed. She tucked them into bed and then with a great flourish, threw a handful of stardust over them which sparkled in the light before settling on their pyjamas. Actually it was talcum powder. Grandmother Mabel was fresh out of stardust. She hadn't been collecting in a while.

The winter days wore on, grey days too cold even to venture outside. Grandmother Mabel developed a cough. Florence and David had streaming colds which lasted three days and three nights but it was Grandmother Mabel's cold that lasted longest. One day she shivered a great deal. Another her hands turned blue and, as the children stared at her face by the light of the open fire, it seemed she was paler now, older by a century or more. The light of the flames still danced in the two dark currants of her eyes. Her hair was still snow white and her voice the sound of candy floss. But she was fading away. Her time with them was drawing to a close.

One morning, when the blackbirds outside the window

draped strings of song over the laurel hedge and Pee-po the cat set off on patrol across Big Marsh-meadow grandmother Mabel's eyes were closed when they went to kiss her good morning and they wouldn't open even when they both kissed her again.

'She's dead,' said David, his eyes twin goldfish bowls of tears.

'No silly, she's just sleeping. Let's make breakfast and we'll think of what to do.'

Florence suggested going over to Mr Dewey's house. He was their neighbour who lived five fields away. Mr Dewey used to be their father's friend and had a laugh like a foghorn. David was quiet, listening for some answer from within.

'I'm going down to the Hollow,' he said.

'It's not the right time,' said Florence, embarrassed by her brother's remark.

'It's the right thing to do,' replied David, already heading for the hallway where he put on his coat and a pair of green gumboots.

It had snowed overnight but there were footprints and trackmarks all the way across the field – signs that a business of field mice had migrated towards the horse trough – very late in the year for them to be out and about. There were stab marks where an investigating thrush had been poking around for worms and the impressions of a fox's pads showing where it had kept close to the hedge, probably having failed to tunnel under the fence around the hen-run.

A solitary jay rose in a flap from the branch of dead elm.

'Jay,' said David who started to cry again. Florence took him into the fold of her cloak and glued together they trudged through the small drifts of snow towards the hollow.

David set to work the moment they arrived. He started chipping away at the ice at the edge of the pond with a small hammer he produced from his pocket.

He chipped away, on his knees now, his face pink from the effort.

'At last,' he said and delved into the pocket of his duffle coat. He produced a little jar and reached it down into the hole he had punctured into the surface of the pond.

'Where did you get that?' asked Florence.

'Look,' said David, holding up the small jar which slopped with its few inches of water. 'It's summer water.' And indeed, as David held up the jar, with the sun behind, Florence thought she could see flashes of summer lightning as the water caught the sun's rays and she imagined she could smell wild flowers – the thin scents of stitchwort and the green smell of cow parsley.

Back home, David used an unfamiliar word as he traced a thin wash of water over Grandmother Mabel's eyes.

'With this summer water I anoint you.' With his free hand he was holding Florence's hand which trembled slightly in his grip. Nothing happened, at least not right away . . .

But that night, after they had had a supper of cheese on toast and fed the cats and put fresh hay out for the horses they went to look at grandmother's body but the bed was empty.

Earlier that evening Mr Dewey, worn out from stacking turnips in his shed had taken a break from his hard labours. Leaning against the gate he had seen the shape of an old woman walking across the field with a spring in her step. It looked like Grandmother Mabel but he couldn't be sure in the dim light and besides she looked as if she was only wearing a summer dress.

He shouted out her name but the woman didn't turn as she walked straight on into the hollow in the woods. But as he turned back to his turnips he swore he heard the twittering of a swallow and there, in the sky, in the very middle of winter was indeed a swallow, its small wings beating furiously, a late bird heading for the far south.

Cassie's Revenge Tragedy

Cassie Hughes was sitting in the utility room sharpening a pair of garden shears in order to exact a terrible revenge on her husband Harry. He had run off with a bit of peroxide nonsense called Poppaline and with that, thirty years of marriage, the bringing up of two children, and enough happy memories to fill a bus had been wiped out as if they had never been. She ran the grey sharpening stone over the blades of the shears, which glistened menacingly, especially when she wetted the stone with her spittle. She placed the shears carefully, ceremoniously even, in a pink holdall and then added a pair of secateurs, just to be on the safe side.

She parked the car at the end of Thornhill Drive, right next to the allotments where Harry spent nearly all his spare time. The sun was just setting and light reflected off the glass, polythene and zinc sheeting of the sheds. It looked like a South American shanty town going to sleep for the night. A few late gardeners were sprinkling water over the vegetable patches, taking advantage of the cooling evening air. Cassie peered through the windscreen, trying to spot Harry, and patted the holdall on the passenger seat.

Harry's shed was easy to find. It was painted pink and blue like a seaside hut. Harry had always been an individualist. The vegetables and flowers he grew reflected this streak in him. He encouraged exotica – aubergines and fat Jerusalem artichokes, things on vines and fruit which looked as if they came from outer space. Even when he wasn't working on the plot he was reading books about gardening or designing things, like the Heath Robinson-style tomato frames, which looked chaotic but which worked like magic. Harry's tomatoes produced the biggest fruit for miles and miles, hanging red and pregnant on their stems. Harry's eyes would glaze over with pride just thinking about them – and he could certainly never bring himself to put one in a sandwich.

Cassie set to work. She began with the climbers which decorated the shed, cutting through the stems of passion flowers and wisteria, cutting only a few inches above the soil so that the damage was invisible. She imagined the plants in a few weeks' time – hanging there, brown and withered, and felt a twinge of sympathy. But then she remembered the peroxide bob of hair and the red slash of lipstick across Poppaline's mouth and she was off again.

As Cassie lopped off all the heads of her husband's dahlias she wasn't to know that he would have a bloomin' enormous heart attack and almost die. She knew – even as she lopped off the blooms called Mariners' Light and snipped conclusively at the Golden Turban and Hamari Dream that she was doing more than wounding him. She was cutting him to the quick, wherever that was. Snip she went, with the confidence of a surgeon. Snip, snip. And when she surveyed her handiwork, the serried ranks of bald, green stalks and the soil covered with spent petals of a dozen bright shades, she felt complete, almost powerful, standing there in the fading orange sheen of the sunset, secateurs in hand. She took one last swipe with her foot at a clump of eyebright in the rockery before getting back in the car.

Her husband Harry – oh! she was still, in her mind, married to him – was a prize gardener, famed for his big marrows and silken roses. Cassie, conveniently, was a dried flower arranger of no little promise. They had met at a Fantastic Fifties evening down at Sol's nightspot and they had danced till they were weary to Frankie Lane, the Inkspots, all those folk. And they had had a happy marriage – no getting away from it.

Sitting down with a cigarette which tasted, curiously, of vanilla, she started to recall so many good times. How Harry filled the house with flowers on her birthday – so that when she

72

arrived home it was like walking into the middle of a Brazilian carnival. She remembered the look on his face as he took in the look on her face and it was one of amazement and great tenderness. Harry, like so many gardeners, was a very tender man. They laughed so much they almost laughed the breath out of their bodies. And then there was the day when Harry had accidentally burnt down the gazebo when the flames of his enormous autumn bonfire spread like an attack by napalm across the compost heap.

The morning after the destruction of Harry's allotment Cassie got up early. She washed the curtains, brushed the cat, read some poems by Tennyson over breakfast and danced a little jig while hoovering the living room. At ten o'clock her friend Muriel called round to drink coffee and encourage Cassie to look for another man. Muriel had done her research well. She had details of rates for advertising in personal columns, some addresses for singles bars and stuff from upmarket dating agencies. There were some agencies nowadays who could find nice graduates or men of considerable accomplishment and they would send you catalogues with photographs and little life stories which were often as moving as novels. Denied access to the children; wife died whilst on holiday in Greece, the sort of thing. Muriel had got the hots for a man in the back of a catalogue who looked like Harrison Ford and lived in Bradford.

Cassie had a pull of convenient deafness as Muriel hit top speed with her plans. Muriel was too much half the time. One time she went so far as to buy vouchers for private tuition for Cassie's sons, Tudur and Iwan, because she'd heard they were a bit slow. Many people thought Muriel hugely impertinent. They were right. Muriel was impertinent. Just before leaving she told Cassie that she really must pull herself together. Pull herself together. That sounded right. Cassie felt as if pieces of her were scattered over thirty years of marriage. She would pull herself together she thought, as she hung the curtains out on the line.

Just then the phone rang and it was, of all people, Poppaline.

'You'll be feeling satisfied, no doubt, with what you've done.'

'Oh just a spot of tidying, you know,' said Cassie, jauntily, a little thrown by the fact it was her.

'He stood a fair chance of cleaning up at the flower show with some of those heads,' said Poppaline with a bit of a hiss coming through on her esses.

Harry usually won at flower shows. Cassie laughed inwardly as she remembered an incident at the Dugwm Flower Show. At around two o'clock, just after the adjudications, Harry had seen a man scuttling towards the door of the Church Hall with his first-prize-winning marrow under his coat. Drawing on rugby playing skills which had remained dormant for thirty years, Harry had brought the man crashing to the floor with a flying-tackle that would have earned him a place in the team. The marrow, unfortunately, hit the ground with an sonorous 'phlupp' and both men came out of their tousle covered in shrapnel from the exploded vegetable. Cassie couldn't help but emit a little laugh.

Poppaline's crow-like voice cut through like cheese-wire.

'Are you laughing? Really Cassie I didn't realise you had so little sympathy in you. You've destroyed him with your vandalism. All those flowers.'

'He should have taken better care of the things he loved then,' returned Cassie, loading every word.

'But now he won't be going to the show because the man's in hospital. He had a heart attack this morning, when he went down to his little allotment. I hope you're satisfied.'

'Which hospital? How is he? What happened?'

'You dumb woman. You and your bloody secateurs happened. He says he doesn't want to see you. He wanted me to tell you that. Expressly. But I'll give you a ring sometime to let you know if he's all right.'

The click of the receiver going down reverberated around the room. Cassie reached behind a copy of 'David Copperfield' to where the packet of fags lay hidden, ready for just such an emergency.

Soon the kitchen looked as if it had been flooded by dry-ice.

A fug of cigarette smoke gave a soft-edged look to the kitchen units. Cassie looked up the phone numbers of all the local hospitals and wrote them down on a pad.

In the first place she tried she got through to an Indian sounding lady in admissions. Cassie was asked if she was a relative and when she explained that she used to be married to Mr Hughes the lady promptly said that she was sorry, but they couldn't give out information about patients to just anybody. That one hurt like a knife. Just anybody?

Defeated, Cassie couldn't bring herself to ring any more hospitals, so she sat on tenterhooks, curiously very much alive because of what was going on.

The phone didn't ring for two days and when it did it was as much as Cassie could do to hold the receiver to her ear, so badly was she shaking. Poppaline sounded gloating as she explained that things had taken a turn for the worse and that Harry was on a drip and just this side of moving into intensive care. There had been, as they say, complications. It was now a matter of prayer and hope and Poppaline hoped that Cassie was happy. Poppaline's voice dropped an octave into a more malicious register and offered up her pièce de resistance. Harry'd opened his eyes the previous evening – just for a few seconds – and had whispered, croakingly, 'My dahlias'. Those might be his very last words, Poppaline has suggested before putting down the phone.

How Cassie regretted allowing Harry to go on that trip to Amsterdam bulb fields where he came under the spell of that sordid witch. Poppaline was a great tulip enthusiast. She was also a man-eater, famed the length and breadth of Dyfed for her huge appetite. Harry, poor dab, hadn't stood a chance, didn't know what hit him.

So Cassie drank that night, cruising her way through what was left of a bottle of gin and making a fair dent in a bottle of vermouth. She watched the fingers of the clock slow down, picked up magazines, put them down again and felt as low as low can be.

Bu then she did what she often did under stress. She decided to bake a cake. She didn't need tranquillisers; didn't even need the gin, although she did like a slurp from time to time. With a cake she was calm, and tonight she would make her favourite date-and-walnut slice, with a whole packet of walnuts if needs be. No scrimping. She loved to eat the cake fresh from the oven and would place it in a pool of evaporated milk and dust it with icing sugar. Cassie's sweet tooth was famous, notorious even. Most people were surprised she had any teeth at all.

As she measured out the ingredients she remembered how Iwan and Tudur when they were little twts would wait excitedly at the end of the kitchen table for the mixing bowl. They would run their fingers around it to get at the very last scraps and then lick the mixing spoon. Neither of them liked the resulting cake but they loved the mixture.

Cassie broke a beautiful free-range egg and thought, for some strange reason, of Poppaline with a bald head, with no hair at all – just a bald white skull – as fragile as an egg-shell. Cassie broke another egg and then another and another, with a growing grin, until she was forced to double the ingredients just to mop up the slop.

She sat next to the Aga for the whole time it took the cake to bake. Her hands seemed to be shaped for prayer although all she actually did was think of her time in the garden wrecking all of Harry's work, all the pain she'd inflicted on those poor plants – if plants do, indeed, feel pain. She felt regret wash over her like the wave of warmth coming out of the oven as she lifted the perfect slab out of the rack.

She was just opening a tin of milk when the phone rang. It was half past five in the morning. Cassie's heart jumped and a series of grim thoughts sped in procession through her mind. She heard Harry's voice.

'What the hell did you do that for. Cut down all my dahlias? I come back from a business trip to find you've cut the bloomin lot down. You even slashed my fine show of Chimbarazo and that was a dahlia and a half.'

A business trip! So the bloody woman had been lying all along. Mixed with her relief that Harry was fine was a complete disbelief that Poppaline could have made up all those lies and so very comprehensively. When Harry found out about her deceit, and all the pain Cassie'd been through, he would be furious. So furious in fact that for a moment Cassie imagined him standing in the garden outside, this handsome man tending the fuschias, trimming the beans, back in their own garden, where he belonged.

The Dean's Last Day

We're outside the window of Number Three, Golgotha Row, and we're zooming in to see the Shakes – an oddball, clean-off sort of family, the sort that could do with a job-lot lobotomy just to make the neighbourhood safe. Down to business. There's Dean Shake, breeder of pit bulls and part time psycho, and his wife Cilla, who hosts Kinkytime parties when her husband's away. She invites the neighbours round, demonstrating the latest line in Taiwanese vibrators and pump-action dildos, makes a fair few hard bob. And there are the kids, Andrea aged eleven and Special Brew, aged eight. A houseful all right. A nightmare's worth if you got on the wrong side of their front door. Where we are now, having invisibly crept through walls.

The dogs are in the kitchen, baying and snarling over a pile of condemned chicken giblets. They're worth a whack of hard cash, killer breeds with fangs like 'Alien' or 'Predator 3'. They hate Dean mainly because they hate chicken giblets.

The dogs never leave the kitchen, other than when one of them gets a steel noose around the neck and is yanked into the back of a van outside. A hundred and fifty quid's worth of mean. The latest scam in the valley is to load a few dogs into the back of an articulated lorry and drive onto the motorway. Then cram on board as many as fifty blokes, placing big bets as the dogs fight in a makeshift ring. One of the dogs has to die along the way, its pain tangled corpse dumped at speed along the central reservation. You feel sometimes that civilisation has packed its bags and left Cwm Berw.

There is supper on the table, meatballs and a side salad of 'Pot Noodle'. It's the sort of unchanging diet that invites rickets and other textbook diseases. Growing up the wrong way. Brew has a dodgy thyroid which has pumped him up a few inches too many. He's had surgery to insert a bit of NHS metal into his skull to stop it from crumbling apart. Bit of a looker, he is, like something that dropped off the back of a meteorite. Worse still, he is, quite simply an Adonis compared with his darling sister.

One day she inadvertently walked into the kitchen. They had to use the noose to get her out.

There's nothing on the television in the corner of the living room, which is unusual. Usually the set is covered with congealing food, pebbledashed there after one of the Dean's cider-induced tantrums. He likes flinging food around. It makes him feel good, fell tough, in command. He's downed a river's worth of gut-rot scrumpy in his time, and the permanent pain in his head has run a deep furrow down his forehead, as if he's had a to-do with an axe-murderer.

It is half past nine in the morning. Dean admires his cowboy boots he thinks gleam like an Arab's teeth. He strides out of the door. He is not to know that this will be his last ever session on the pop.

The moment he walks out the door his name changes. He becomes The Dean, the definite article.

Edit. Dreamy harp music suggesting a span of time elapsed.

A clear February light defines the sides of the buildings outside the courtroom. A raven cronks its way over the nearby church, a black portent. The inquest is due to start in five minutes. Not enough time for a sneaky Bensons before entering the non-smoking precincts of the courtroom. But many members of the courtroom flock have already loaded up on nicotine. The hall outside looks as if a dry ice machine has been at work.

The people in the high ceilinged room aren't working class. They are underclass – stripped of dignity at birth and then given no breaks. Ever. They wouldn't look out of place in the transgalactic bar in 'Star Wars'.

Their general flesh-tint is 'Mothers Pride' white, a pasty

79

bread complexion. The men have faces which describe the spectrum from mortuary white to raging beetroot, a colour scheme which reflects their different drinking regimes. The beer-swillers, some of them in the power-drinking bracket, have distended bellies and jowls like guinea-fowl. Some of the spirit men are wire thin and are as white as sheets while others, weaned on Scotch have pitted noses and smell of peat. Some cough, some fart, some assortment.

The women in the courtroom are dressed in colours out of a Draylon furniture catalogue – Dead Olive, Matt Purple and Indescribable Fuschia. Some have perms or demi-perms which look as if they've been achieved by applying a paste of flour and water, or worse still, by a discount store spray of horse bone glue.

The coroner, Howard Beth, known locally as Mortis, shuffles in looking like a cockroach. He suffers from advanced arthritis and his forehead, which slopes backwards just above the eyebrows, makes him look like one of those Cro-Magnon types. This lack of occipital lobes, those twin seats of the imagination, is complemented by a lack of cheekbones. His face looks as if the Open Cast sank it for him. This is one weird looking coroner.

He makes monthly appearances at Llanilltyd court. Usually it's suicides – courtesy of Martini and aspirin; two bar electric fires being hugged to death in the bath; hanging on rafters, using baling twine or leather belts; pipes leading from exhausts through car windows and drowning, which Beth imagines to be the most horrible and the most desperate.

Mortis coughs, rattling a glob of phlegm, and kicks off. He talks in a sub dialect of Public Servant, full of sub clauses and qualifiers. Nobody knows what the hell he's on about, but judging from the state on the boy he won't be around long enough to make a difference. The quite literally staggering tale of the Dean's last day on earth emerges.

Dean Shake, as we know, went drinking. September 15th, 1991, overcast. During the day's binge he sustained a number of blows to the head. The court was particularly concerned with finding out which particular blow had been the fatal one.

He caught the Shoppabus at ten o'clock, and by half past ten he was necking his first bitter. By half past two he was being bounced out of a wedding party after making a dick of himself. This was at the Alpine Retreat, a misnomer of a place, nestling as it does behind a builders' merchants – which does admittedly have a mountain of sand in the yard and within deafening earshot of a small family foundry, which never shuts, even on Christmas Day. On being thrown out through the Retreat's front doors he stumbled backwards – his head bouncing on the lawn. He was soon on his feet, however, yelling oaths in vigorous Anglo-Saxon on his way to the next drinking clinic.

Which was the 'Whatnot', a pub with the homeliness of the Black Hole of Calcutta. This was, still is, a frenetic exchange for hot goods and bad drugs. Prostitutes clip their nails there, itinerants cash their Giros, faded businessmen close their last deals and there is often blood on the floor. In an argument over an obscure rule of the game Dean was slugged over the head with a pool cue. The second blow.

Next to take the stand was a taxi driver called Marvin Gaye, yes, named after the Motown recording star.

Marvin had grown up to be a Zeppelin sized affair with lager breasts and an ability to crease clothes from the inside out. He is a man fair lapped in fat and could withstand polar winds, an ability of limited use to a man who hasn't ventured further north than Llandeilo.

Marvin makes furniture breathless.

Marvin received a call to pick up the Dean at eleven thirty. He arrived at the Massam Tandoori takeaway in Scurvy Street at twenty to twelve. The Dean had reached the stage in his inebriation where he had stopped communicating in English and had switched to some other language altogether. Wolof maybe, with a hint of Basque. He insulted the other customers and swung a punch at one, but it was an ineffectual flailing, which served only to dislodge a calendar and startle the coolie loaches in the aquarium.

The Dean had gone into slow motion over the ten yards between the takeaway and the taxi and while Marvin held open the door, the Dean laboriously manhandled the aluminium foil containers, sloshing curry over the back seat. The stains are there to this day. You just can't shift turmeric. The Dean fell backwards, the hard connecting of skull and pavement making an audible crack.

Marvin had come close to thrombosis in lifting him back into the car. By the time they'd reached Orchid Close the Dean seemed more lucid, pontificating on life, how it was all a farkin joke and fark he could farkin murder a farkin lager.

The next witness was the next door neighbour, Betty Evans, single – a point she makes in Mortis' direction, stressing it with a lascivious sneer. She took up the story of the Dean's gallant if zigzagging trek to the front door, weaving then falling, yes she had seen him fall but no she couldn't say for certain he had banged his head because they'd just had a new dividing wall built between the two gardens.

With everybody's breakfast now well settled it was time for the pathologist's report. The man was small and jerky. He nervously described the process of making an incision at the back of the head, then peeling away the skin to show the principal contusions. Essential details were given such as the weight of the principal organs. The heart weighed such and such while the state of the liver was outlined. He then pronounced the genitalia as being normal which caused the Dean's common law wife Cilla to tell her friend Kelvey, 'I could have told him that.' Her voice cut across the courtroom and detonated some firecracker laughter.

It was then Cilla's turn to act the witness. A peroxide blonde sporting tattoos which proclaimed her football fan allegiance to the 'Swans' and on her fingers such tags as 'love' and 'hate' and on her neck, intriguingly, the single word 'Marrakesh'. She teetered up to the stand on a pair of cracked gold high heels, having the autumnal look of the recently widowed, set off to dramatic effect by half gloves of nicotine staining.

Dean had lurched through the back door in the middle of 'Prisoner Cell Block H', must have been going on for half twelve. He had dumped the Indian on the table and announced he was going upstairs for a dump. He had only managed to get half way up the stairs when he fell backwards and landed with a crash on the hall carpet.

Cilla found him face up, having difficulty with his breathing. Did she attempt to revive him in any way? Yes, m'lud, she had stroked his earlobes. Where had she picked up that particular first aid tip? In a magazine m'lud.

Then a chunk of time disappeared. Cilla didn't phone for an ambulance for quite some time. The ambulance crew had testified that they arrived at half past three, the usual journey time from the hospital to the estate being some fifteen minutes. The Dean had died on that short journey. So why the delay? Dunno. What had happened in that time? Not a lot. Did you do anything beyond stroke your common law husband's earlobes? Don't think so. Then, the dawn of realisation. Did Mr Shake eat his curry? No, I did. While Dean Shake, the Dean himself lay in the hallway struggling for his very life Cilla had eaten his Chicken Dhansak and a cold keema nan.

Cilla felt guilt well up inside her. It agitated her face muscles. She made a decision. She would never, ever eat Chicken Dhansak again. It would be a sort of memorial to Dean. Besides, the lentils made her fart like a duck.

The Case for Critics

When Melissa was eight, at pretty much every practice-hour, her mother would exhort her that she really must be careful, else she'd have someone's eye out with that violin bow. Or worse, darling. She mustn't use her bow-arm with so much gusto. Swing so wild. Anyone would have thought she'd been brought up in an Alabama swamp.

Her mother's voice, in memory, as in life, had a sherry slur. Most every day, hers was a medium-dry speech disorder.

Today Mel was standing in a hotel room which commanded an expansive and expensive view of inky sea stretching away towards Naples. She had a thrilling room done out in primary colours – yellow walls straight out of Van Gogh and a perfect Mondrian-blue ceiling without a blemish or air-blister. Normally Melissa would have found such a colour scheme too challenging. But today she was feeling like a goddess. Her signature on the hotel checking-in book had been bold and assertive, not her usual tight little sea-horse.

She looked at herself in the full-length mirror. Under her arm she was toting, yes, that was the word, toting a machine gun.

Normally she carried her violin case with her everywhere she went, including the loo. But not today. Today she'd given it to the airline to carry – less hassle after a four month stint on the circuit. The Lutoslawski memorial gig in Warsaw. Dvorak in Seattle. Mahler all over the place. Draining. All cities melding as one, a blur of taxis and accents, skyscrapers reflecting skyscrapers.

It had been an afternoon shot through with complete panic. She'd stood for half an hour watching the luggage carousel going round and round. There was a sense of grief, of losing a partner and she had sobbed as she spoke to the Alitalia lady – who strained to hear what she was saying, or, indeed, failed entirely to understand her Derbyshire lilt. The woman said she'd ring the hotel the moment they had news and hoped Melissa had an enjoyable concert that evening. Melissa thanked her. Then she thought, how stupid! The south Italian air seemed to come off the tip of a blowlamp. She wouldn't even be able to play tonight. Not without her Guanerius, her perfect partner for Pergolesi.

Melissa lifted the stock to her shoulder. It was heavy but not cumbersome, and she found she could tuck the little nub-handle under her chin as easily as her violin. She took aim and with a ridiculous, a disarming lucidity saw, in her mind's eye . . . Henderson. He was the bulbous nosed and mean-spirited music critic of the Washington Post and she imagined him taking his usual concert seat, his critical acumen drenched, as usual, in fiery bourbon. He looked at her once, as he always did. Just once. As if she didn't exist. As if he were the true artist and Melissa just a smell under the rim of his nostril. He paid full, straight-backed, adrenaline charged attention when he saw that tonight she wasn't carrying a violin but rather a squat, compact sub-machine gun, probably an Uzi. When he saw her taking aim, Fat Boy started running up the aisle. But too late, sunshine! The first violin, assuming combat stance, sprayed him with hundreds of bullets, a blood-bespattered sonata, as his body fell crumpedly. And Mel had a feeling of complete satisfaction, a, well, satiation of spirit, as she saw the little pig-man drop to his knees and finally sprawl. He had cost her a place in the major league. Now he, supine, danced a ridiculous little dance in time to no time at all and expired. Mel ran her trigger finger along the warm barrel. And then a thought occurred to her. That critic from the New York Times. What had he said about her Sibelius last year? Something about lacklustre and an insult to Finland. He had better start watching his shadow, thought Melissa, gently cradling the instrument back into the velvet of the case.

She would be catching the next plane home.

She managed to hide the machine-gun in the freight container, by placing it in a case for a French horn she bought in a little smoky music shop she often visited in the old part of the town. This made sure it wouldn't have to pass the metal detectors. The only people who searched the freight containers were looking for drugs. The orchestra's last-but-one principal bassoonist was caught that way, smuggling a large block of hashish from Turkey. She still sent him letters in prison, but he never replied.

The gun, she thought, was beautiful. It was also the most popular sub-machine gun in the world. The Uzi, beloved of terrorists the world over. Mel liked the fact that, like a musical instrument, it too had a history. Obvious really, but not the sort of thing she'd ever thought about. But her new book told her everything she needed to know. Weight, 3.5 kgs. The length. The muzzle velocity. When the Brits handed over Palestine and the state of Israel was born the Israelis needed a gun to arm an entire populace. In the Fifties a Major, Major Ouzel Gal, had come up with this squat, six hundred rounds per minute dreamy little handgun. They were now made in Holland under licence: sell like hot cakes, outstripping all other machine gun sales in the Western world. And Mel had one. And Mel was taking it home with her. She wasn't entirely clear why. Bloodlust. Revenge. Not motives you'd associate with the toast of the conservatoire.

Cyprus was becoming an essential island-hop for major-league assassins like Adad who arrived with the floral-shirted holidaymakers and lager louts. He had just checked that his Cayman islands account was full to the brim with Iranian money before setting off on the next leg of his journey. This was Adad's last gig. He was bored, or satiated, or maybe it was simply that his bad conscience was rebelling against so much blood. Blood drenched his life and he could hear the mullahs' cries ringing in his ears with every death. He was in their pay and he heard them, even in sleep, exhorting him on and on, for the cause and against the spreading cancer of the West. He found their out-and-out frenzy gave him migraines. Hate this. Hate that.

They were so unutterably irrational. He, for one, quite liked pop music – couldn't see that much harm in it. Adad loved the latest 'Prince' album and listened to it on headphones on his way to work. But the mullahs, with their M1 carbines, chanting and screaming on the squares of Tehran, didn't give a toss for the stunning harmonies of great songs like 'When Doves Cry'. And his great guitar licks. Their loss, misguided buggers.

There were times when Adad worried, most seriously indeed, about becoming so Westernized he'd end up on someone else's hit-list.

Adad arrived in London just as dawn was lighting up the wet tarmac of the runways. He knew his passport would pass muster. It had been designed by a guy who used to be payrolled by the CIA.

He got a taxi into the city and checked into the hotel room. A man with the same build, same clothes had been living there for the past few days. When the police came looking for new Arabs in town he'd be long gone, riding Continental to South Carolina via Boston. He'd be picked up in JFK. He'd be picked up in Dallas. But there were places where even the customs' men were on the Ayatollah's payroll. The guy was all pervasive.

The hit was due at eight. He had the target's name and a definite location. His family had been taken care of. They would be in a school meeting.

There was a Hertz car to take him. Adad knew London as well as he did twenty other cities. The hire car had been rented by a fall guy, who'd retire on what he was getting paid, and had only to deny all knowledge of anything whatsoever and claim that his car had been stolen. Easy scam for easy money. At five to eight Adad parked under a lime tree. He went up to the front door. As the man, Blythe, answered the door, Adad flipped open the case. He'd always been a casual operator. Inside there was a violin. Why hadn't he noticed the difference in weight? His nerve fled like a high note. He saw the victim's gun coming up through a series of freeze-frames, the dead-cool in his eyes taking in Adad's life as if it was his own. Which, with a casual palping of the trigger, it was.

That night, in Madison, Mel played an elegy as if the audience was made up of all the dead of Passchendaele. Or Cambodia. Didn't know why. Didn't know why this elegy. But the audience wept. Felt they'd heard Paganini play just after he sold his soul to the devil. Yeah, sure as daisy, that's what Paganini would have played. Possessed. Bathed in sweat. Each note terminal, as if it would never be played again. Not in this life.

Dying Days

Billy Gwilym, known as Gwil, loved estuaries and judging by the X-ray he was now turning into one. The black and white pattern on the doctor's plate looked like an aerial shot of his beloved Gwendraeth, its salt creeks radiating out and away from the widening tract of the river. As if to complete the conceit, Gwil's lungs, on cue, whistled like the wigeon ducks that would sight the river from on high. These were birds which lawnmowered the purslane and spartina grass, their calls wild and aerated, like wind scything across. Whee-oo!

But the wild sound of Gwils' lungs was the sound of tortured alveolae, the sound of a clogging, angry emphysema with a garnish of bronchitis, as if disease was making a meal of him.

Here was a man who measured out his life, not in coffee spoons, but in cigarettes, with far too many smoked with the filters ripped off. Add to that the years when tired veins silted up with a catalogue of fats – some lipid, some polyunsaturated, a tide of clinging globules. The alluvium of life.

The doctor's eyes steadfastly refused to meet Gwil's bloodshot pair.

'Break it to me gently,' said Gwil, with a real rasper of a cough, the sort that breaks out like rimshot in isolation wards.

'If I were you I'd get a gun and shoot myself.'

'If that's you being gentle, remind me not to come to you if I'm taken seriously ill.'

'I'm a realist Mr Gwilym. You are seriously ill.'

'And you're burying me. So what about some comforting words of advice. I thought you were meant to dish out that sort of stuff along with the pills.'

'Advice. Well. Now, let's see. If I were you . . . ' The doctor's gaze fled around the room.

'Yes,' said Gwil, his illness speckled eyes out on their stalks.

' . . . I'd throw one hell of a party.'

'A party?'

'Yes, a sort of leaving do,' said the doctor, helpfully.

'When exactly?'

'Oh, this side of a fortnight. You've got about that long.'

Gwil trudged home, hunchbacked by the news, aware of the sound of a sand-timer running. He took the short cut through the arboretum, to save time. To save time! He almost laughed at the irony of that, but chose to weep awhile instead.

He rested on the stump of a Swedish whitebeam, taking in the view of the river which glinted in the late sun, a red thread cutting through green fields. There had been days when just sitting here would lift him high, moments of transcendence.

Now death denied him such future epiphanies. Death, that inescapable old sand timer.

Gwil sat among the Himalayan firs, stunted mountain species which grew sideways. He looked up at Atlas cedars, crabapples bonsaied by age, bird cherries, dwarf redwoods. He sat among them for the very last time and the sadness washed over him like a grey mist.

The doomed man lit a cigarette. He had to struggle to get enough of a rhythm going to suck the smoke into the worn rubber bags of his lungs, into the clogged estuary on the photographic plate.

In the distance Gwil could see the Dutch gable house, built by the dyke builders who had first reclaimed the fields from the sea and made a triangle of the estuary mud-flats. The one on the left was the house where his mother was born: the house on the right was the one where his father had lived. And beyond was the chromium river, moving out inexorably to the small waves and regular breakers. Beyond the sound of the wildfowlers' guns which made a cotton wooled sound at this distance. Phlump! Phlump!

The cigarette tar drained down like sump oil into the darker recesses of his body cavity. He threw the butt away. Too late to give up now. His friend Titchy used to say 'You'll never save enough coupons to buy yourself an iron lung.' The bastard. Gwil chuckled to himself. Time for action.

He stopped at the house to pick up his building society book and caught the bus into town. He had to see the manager to empty the account at one fell swoop. With his life savings (that was a good one) safe in an old school satchel he walked onto the forecourt of Bevins. The luxury cars gleamed, burnished metal bonnets, Simonised sides reflecting the purposeful strides he made up to the salesroom.

Two unctuous assistants homed in on him from opposite corners with Exocet straightness.

'What does sir have in mind?'

Gwil found the words 'impending death' forming on his lips but stated, baldly and boldly:

'Mercedes sports. The white one, with dark navy leather trim. I'd like it please.'

'Would you like to test drive it sir? Lovely day for it.'

'No thanks.'

'Would you like to talk to Mr Bevins about repayment options. He'll be free in a jiff.'

'No thanks, I'll be paying cash.'

Gwil put the bag on the desk.

He nursed the car up to a ton, in the middle lane of the motorway. No point in running it in. He drove it down to the beach, took it skittering along the surf line before heading for home.

'How did it go, Gwil?' asked his wife, who was waiting at the front gate.

Gwil nodded in the direction of the car which made three shrill bleeps as the alarm kicked in.

Gwil's wife looked at the car and understood. He'd always said 'Before I die I want to drive . . . '

The Mercedes sports accelerated fast enough to make Gwil

and his wife feel like astronauts. In the morning they drove as far as Reading on the motorway and then looped back home.

That afternoon Gwil did a round of people he knew. First he went round to Jimmy Dean's. When the red faced old greaser answered the door Gwil spun round on the ball of his foot and gave him a right hook which would have floored Marvin Hagler. Jimmy fell like a sack of spuds. Twenty two and a half years ago Jimmy had had a fling with Gwil's wife. Payback time. Gwil tidied up a good few other matters that afternoon – minor revenges, but it wasn't all vendetta material. He filled the car with flowers from Mrs McGaskeys nursery and took them round to relatives, friends. When he arrived at the local hospital he was so weighted down with bunches of gladioli that a male nurse offered him the use of a stretcher to wheel them around. And then on the Thursday afternoon, as a wash of fine rain drifted in from the hills, Gwil made a pact with the Devil.

You could tell from the way he was dressed that this was an afternoon of some import. Gwil had on his best suit, a classy demob number that had come back into fashion only that year. As he strode to the car he felt like a million dollars, a curious feeling for a man whose body was riddled with ripening and deadly cells. He gunned his glorious high performance car, running through all the gears in ten seconds, allowing the purr of the engine to mix with the sound of headwind bouncing off the bonnet. He managed a hundred and twenty on the dual carriageway en route to the Devil's house. Gwil, having made his mind up, was eager as bees to sell his soul, to buy some extra time on earth.

The Devil lived in a tumbledown house on the edge of town, an old miner's place. Anyone in any doubt that this was the real Devil, who thought this might be any old demonic imposter, might do well to remember the tale of the three lads who went round there to play trick or treat one Halloween. Two of them had been rendered deaf and mute, only the scaredness in their eyes giving a hint of the horrors they had seen. The other lad, who'd had the temerity to peer in through the window, had been turned into a lump of charcoal and even though the Devil had been arrested amid talk of laser guns and strange apparatus there hadn't been scrap of evidence against him. The local coroner, Vincent Wax, settled for an unusual explanation – self combustion, the first case he had come across.

Gwil marched across the yard, which was littered with the rusty hulks of scrap cars, tangles of old barbed wire and briars. He knocked on the door and a man half his height with the most piercing green eyes – a bright iguana green – met his gaze.

'Come in,' said the Devil. 'You're late.'

Gwil accepted the tumbler of whisky offered him and sat on the edge of the chair proffered by Old Nick himself.

'Right then, Mr Gwilym. What's the trade?'

Gwil told him, straight up. He fixed the Devil with a poker player's eyes, slits which gave nothing away.

'I'll give you my soul . . . '

'That's where we usually begin with these things . . . ' said the devil, stifling a yawn.

'If you'll give me the usual span. Three score years and ten.'

'There you go, quoting that fairy tale book again.'

'That's the deal. No hidden extras.'

'I'm afraid that's not enough. Or at least it is enough but it's too straightforward, what with you thinking that offering your soul for ever and a day is a bargain, which it is, until you begin to comprehend eternity. So let's talk maths.'

The Devil took a burnt piece of wood out of the fire and drew a circle on the floor.

'There are those who say that infinity occurs when the arc of a circle of infinite radius becomes a straight line.'

Like a teacher the Devil pointed at the features in turn – the section of the circle's rim which was the arc and showed how the arc straightened as the circle grew.

Gwil found himself struggling to deal with the abstraction before him even as the Devil talked about how many people imagined the circle had to break whilst others saw it flipping in on itself, making a figure eight.

'That's the scale of what you're suggesting. An infinity of time is eternity and I'll own you for all that. Are you game for it? Are a few measly years in the company of your wretched friends and doomed companions worth the trade?'

Gwil sipped the whisky which glowed amber in the fireplace light. The Devil's eyes were inscrutable. A clock ticked somewhere, sounding louder now, more insistent.

'Yes,' said Gwil, picking up his coat. 'I think they're worth it.'

'It's a deal then.'

As Gwil took his leave the Devil proferred a limp hand. Gwil shook it, surprised to feel a human warmth. Walking back towards the Merc he was even more surprised to hear the Devil shouting after him:

'Drive carefully, now. Drive carefully.'

Bad Eating

Drop down, tilt down, passing through the hazy gases of the late twentieth century stratosphere, burst the light and identify beneath you green country and a road cutting through. As you swing down to ground level clock a grey car heading west at eighty maybe more miles per hour. On either side of the road a dead marsh extends. And listen, listen and you can hear some real painful banjo playing, like the player's fingers are going through a cheese grater. This is missing chromosome country, Boondocks Central, and the hicks are out there, all around, beyond the marshes and they are growing fatter and more stupid with every passing millisecond, saturated on their fatty hatred of all other life, of anything they cannot begin to understand.

This is an extraordinary car, with an extraordinary passenger. Inside the car is the restaurateur from-hell, Oscar Flambé heading for the next eaterie which fate, nudging a podgy finger to its place on the map, has earmarked for Grognant, a little town just round the back of beyond. As he folds the map a small tattoo is revealed on his wrist which reveals the tag 'Eat and Die'.

Oscar is a man whose exo-skeleton has been wrapped around with layer after layer of top-quality fat, pig-dripping maybe. He is leaning back into the leatherette seat and rolling the name, mispronouncedly on his palpy lips. 'Grugnont'. He takes a cigar out of his breast pocket, licks its side, then, abruptly and eardrum-piercingly, shouts at his assistant, Grimbley, who is doing the driving. Grimbley, from the back, looks like an escapee from a Dickens' asylum. He looks the same from the front.

'What did you forget this morning you pile of human ordure?'

Grimbley's none-too-agile mind limps back to the morning, when he'd taken his praying mantis frame out to the garage, dusted a handkerchief over the Simonised hood of the brown Austin Cambridge. He put the hamper down, opened the door, started her up and she glided out of the garage like a barge slinking along a canal. Fu-urk! The hamper! The hamper was back there, and his nibs coming up to feed-time, which in his case is never very far away.

Luckily Oscar had brought along a box of experimental fruit – guyabanas, tamarinds and bullet-shaped lychees which he started eating as the car snaked through Swindon with its mirror plated skyscrapers endlessly reflecting each other. By the half-way mark of the journey the back seat was a fly-trap of extraordinary stickiness. Oscar, his jaws working like twin pistons, pulped and mulched and gulped the exotic harvest like a slow food processor. This was seventh heaven for him, eating crescents of watermelon with busy, rabbit teeth. In his mind he was adding strong liqueurs to the fruity mulch, inventing an array of brand spanking new cocktails. The first would be called 'Oscar'; a bowl-you-over, big-as-big-can-be drink, with an architecture of straws and plastic dangling monkeys.

They stopped in a Petite Chef, the equivalent, to Oscar's way of thinking, to being skinned alive and dipped in salt. Eating in these places with these slurping people was exquisite torture. He hated the orange salads with their crinkled little figs of fruit and the edge of grease. Osk ordered the chef's special. When it arrived he was jolted out of his seat. He screamed for the manager who arrived wearing a lapel badge which announced 'Hello! My name is Kevin' which seemed like a further insult. Oscar went for the verbal broken bottle assault saying hideous, jagged things and pushing out a finger with every key word. Cesspit. Pox. Ordure-heap. Egg of the month. With every volley 'Hello my name is . . . ' took a step backwards towards the kitchen door, nearer the comfort of the full set of Sabatier knives.

Osk had momentum.

'So who's your chef, Helen Keller? Are they giving Michelin stars for seven kinds of shit nowadays?'

'Hello my name is' looked with anguish at the other customers. They thought the floor show was great and Oscar their hero, articulating all the thoughts they'd had over all those years of stopping off in Petite Chefs.

Oscar continued to warm to the task, 'Hello my name' . . . treading water backward, through the kitchen doors with their little portholes of glass.

Oscar surveyed the cooking arena.

'So this is it! This is the latrine where your team of failed surgeons cut up the meat and crack open the addled eggs. And this, I take it is the sump oil into which the grand parade of dead things drops?'

'I think you'd better leave.'

'Not before meeting the kind of the ordure heap. Come on, which of you illegal aliens is it?'

'Me sir,' said someone who looked like a transvestite Albanian.

'You sir. You are the cooker in this kitchenette?'

'That I am sir.'

'Do you not feel ashamed?'

'Not really. You get what you ask for and the production line works perfectly.'

'But do you not feel as if you'd like to break out, use hot gooseberry sauce, do French, make things at least look attractive?'

'I do.'

'Then come with me,' and Oscar dragged him out into the non-greasy air.

And so the Cooker started his journey to being a good cook, then a chef and then a Blue Riband chef. His heart was, however heavy. He was leaving behind four 'Sunny Server' stars and any chance he would have of getting into bed with Wanda, the

Nigerian student who was on vegetables. Most of the other staff at the Petite were vegetables, but Wanda stood out among them, peeler in hand. Never would he uncork those dark nipples from their holster-strap.

Soon they were in a terrain studded with hills, a greener Tuscany, and Oscar couldn't get over the random arrangement of trees and hedges, which grew where they wanted to, not where Capability Brown and mob planted them. They stopped in the next town and Osk sent Grimbley to fetch a bottle of good tequila. They were drinking fearfully strong strawberry daiquiris as they crossed the border into Wales, at the same time as the drinkers at Grognant's worst pub were beginning to down their pints.

The reason the men who drink at the bar of the Trap hunt is that they are themselves hunted – by shadowy ex-wives, by bad bank balances, by their own troubled consciences. A survey once showed that one in four men had committed crimes that would have merited a prison sentence. They obviously hadn't brought their clipboards round to the Trap – they'd have won maximum points, made the needles of their calculation-charts hit top-graph. Far away from them was the place that Flambé was to send them.

On the rim of the sea, in the lower West of Wales was one of the last big marshes – a remnant of what was once a grand swamp, alive with ploshing hogs and waterbirds. The last bit was an area of waving Phragmites reeds, where once wild boar truffled and cavorted. And now they were back – escapees from a wildlife park where the owner, harangued by despotic tax-men, had topped himself. One morning, the first visitor found the turnstiles open and, being brave, she ventured far enough to find Terence Cleave, upside down and impaled on the railings of the bear-pool, having leaped off the nearest tree like a flying fox without the knack. Before going for the Big Jump, Cleave the Zoo, as he was known locally, had opened every cage door. Many of the animals stubbornly refused the cold, November, Cardiganshire air. But the boars, alive to the drifting pangs of the nearby Chinese takeaway had disappeared like driven spirits, their stumpy legs pounding out the music of escape as they headed for the back of the Chinese takeaway, with its discards of beansprouts and plastic bags of old foo yung.

And seven wolves had escaped, their white snouts taking in each molecule of air, before breaking through the wire. Four of them had found a living – running shotgun-gauntlets, outwitting fox-hunts (fancy thinking that foxhounds could ever outsmart them – wolfhounds, maybe, but foxhounds!) One lithe creature had been pulverised by a lorry, another had failed to understand the danger of a gin-trap (in this day and age, a gin trap) but the other five had held close, obeying the ancient, Transylvanian laws of the pack. They had, however, seen the clear wisdom of not howling. They were now silent wolves, lithe and lethal.

But in a birch wood, seven days after their escape, they strayed into a fusillade of shotguns.

'That's three thousand quid that bloke Flombey, or whatever his name is, owes us. Right boys, let's get these wolves back to base'. The boys from the 'Trap' were fulfilling their contract.

Flambé had a lot of people working for him, spread out right across the country.

A team of dullard oye-boys were rafting their way across to a rocky island of the North Wales coast to collect roseate tern eggs, and even as their overladed tub hove into view of the colony, so a paper explosion of birds came off the island to screech and kirrick above the shaven heads of the robbers. Oscar fancied having the eggs of the most threatened seabird in Europe to make his Flamboyant Souffle. If he was going to have an Armageddon theme to his grand opening night it might as well be the real thing, not some plastic, insipid imitation end-of-the-world do.

He was paying the equivalent of a month's worth of Giros to this gang of nasty skinheads, and they were nasty – their brains pulped by gut-rot scrumpy, their attitudes aligned with Nuremberg.

In other parts of the country kids were looking for dormice for the pot, rare dragonflies so that their wings might be used to garnish fruit cocktails, and old women were assembling sprays of rare plants – bee orchids for corsages, St David's sea-lavender for table decorations and as the central arrangement of the place a big spray made up of Snowdon lilies, an unique arrangement because they are, or were unique, that is until Osk's opening night. Osk loved flowers, wisps of green ferns, rising like steam above his painstaking arrangements, exuberant. The large lipped orchids. The deep violet irises, shot through with distress-flare yellow. Dressy, showy roses, each petal in its place.

Even on the Big Day the builders and decorators were putting finishing touches to the restaurant. Murray Maxwell, in charge of the building side of things, had, two days before the opening, finished some of the outrageous features. There were astonishing pillars and wedding cake tiers of brickwork, like Gaudi buildings transplanted from Barcelona and crammed indoors. Even the brickies, Stan and Eddie Lip, knew they were involved in something extraordinary – like the stone-chisellers at Notre Dame must have felt when looking up, seeing the whole thing grow. Grimbley, Oscar's personal assistant would come through death's door every half an hour to bring them a cup of tea apiece.

Wiard, the Flemish interior designer was decorating as if he were on a mission from God. The furniture he had moved into place was unashamedly Frank Lloyd Wright rip-off – strictly Taliesin period with soft lines melding and flowing. An enormous copy of Oscar's favourite painting, 'The Plains of Heaven' formed a serene backdrop to the big dining room, with its scene of transcendent, beautiful mountains with angles and a sense that here were all the mountains of the world, and the light of all skies, splashed across one canvas.

One wall depicted the very essence of twentieth century joy – big blown up photographs of hostages being released – most being familiar faces, leaving their hell-cells in Lebanon. Gaunt, unbroken, coyly smiling – these were affecting images indeed.

Brian Keenan, astonished by flashbulbs. Waite, lost in a sea of questions. The facing wall was a still, dead orange colour.

The flickering torches of the mad-angry crowd twinkled like the light of a small galaxy pouring itself down the lanes over the hills. They were coming from Dolhafan, Bronllyw, Nwydol, Parwenci, Niwbwl, Garan Ddu, old hatreds, almost genetic, unleashed when they'd heard what was going on in the restaurant in town. This was witch-hunting in the television age, but the anger was centuries old – the anger of those who believe they're right, whatever. There had been rumours. Of course there had been rumours. All those cars coming from London, some even from the Continent to eat there. What could be worth all that money, all that travelling? Light aircraft would bring people in for lunch and that fat man who owned it, what was his name, Flamby, had even built a helicopter landing pad just behind the council offices. How many palms had he greased with silver to get that one through committee? Flamby was in league with the Devil, maybe a first cousin. He had changed the town. Taxi drivers were now disgruntled when they had passengers who didn't give a tip as big as the fare. There was local inflation on a par with Brazil.

To know the reason you'd have to peer in through the slightly steamy windows of the place itself to witness appalledly, what's going on, what's being served up.

It's what Oscar describes as the Very Last Supper with light soufflés made of roseate tern eggs, cold if condemned meats and, God-help-them all, little nibbles which some medical students picked up in the dissection rooms at the local teaching hospital. Spooner, the chef who'd been encouraged to leave the Petite Chef to work with Oscar had slit his wrists with a corkscrew when he'd found out what was going down.

The centrepiece looks suspiciously, stomach churningly like a bake wrapped, sixteen stone man, set in an enormous pastry-weave basket filled with steaming leaf-vegetables. Standing sentinel on either side are two roast wolves, cooked to a traditional Hong Kong dog-recipe, with the addition of lemon-coloured glass eyes to bring the whole thing back to life after its spell in the oven. But it is the centrepiece which has enraged people, made them see white. This human shaped cooked meat has only nine toes. Arwel Evans, late of this parish, buried a week before, had only nine toes. And it only took one visit to the graveyard to find that his grave, a family grave where he was crammed in with three other relatives, had been broken into. The edge-of-frenzy mob was dealing with something quite out of its ken, but it knew how to deal with it.

The following morning all the world had come to the scene of complete carnage that was Shirtville Street, and what had been 'Oscar's Place'. Forensic guys from the Fire Service were sifting through the smouldering mess of charred timbers and torched bodies. Body bags were being stacked up as if in preparation for a Vietnam movie and the death toll reported on the radio rose by the bulletin. They could account for everyone except Oscar. He had, as usual, fled.

So the next time you're dining out in a new place, insist on checking out the manager, or even the chef. If he has a small tattoo on his left wrist, forget it. You'll be eating nightmares. For Oscar is the patron saint of crap restaurants, always on the move, forever opening up.

Eight Life Cat

It was the day when the Hungarian Union of Witches went on strike in Budapest over the new tax system. The same day three small Afghan boys lost limbs after playing with antipersonnel devices disguised as big gaudy plastic butterflies, dropped near their playground by Soviet helicopters. And the day when a man called Cat sorted things out, once and for all. Or at least planned to. But life, as the Innuits say, has a habit of turning the clearest flakes to the darkest mulch.

Cat was a saw-mouthed, scar-cheeked walking oak tree of an ex bare-knuckle prize-fighter who liked nothing more than taking on the local gendarmerie in Pandy after a twenty pint meditation session down at CJ's. This was a saddoes' watering hole which abbreviation was thought by many to stand for Creutzfeld-Jacob, especially after seeing the vegetable matter in human guise that grew on the bar stools, occasionally managing to order another pint of snakebite with a Diamond White 'n' blackcurrant chaser.

There was one bar where there used to be three separate rooms: this helped the barstaff, who needed to know whether they were in the line of fire. But Cat, with his casual way of bringing all disasters down upon himself was the worst customer. Now that the local pigs had wised up and stocked up an arsenal of CS gas and test-trial taser stun-rods, Cat had started drinking with a gas mask to hand and a dustbin lid – his deflective and trusty shield – at his side. He liked the fighting that much. And on the Day of Sorting It Out Cat was feeling like a bear with a sore arse, more specifically a grizzly that's had its ursine haemorrhoids sandblasted before sitting down in the sea.

Yeah, that bad.

He'd just found out about a foursome that had visited Cardiff the previous Friday night when he was out cop-baiting. The group comprised his wife Prudence in company with that scuddy loan shark Stumpy Evans along with his daughter Florence with . . . he could hardly bring himself to think it . . . with a local copper, Martin something, a slightly Scandinavian looking fair-faced youth who still bore the impact mark of a cider flagon Cat had upended and jagged into his cheek more as a demure warning than an object lesson in not messing with the Cat. The four of them. Cardiff. To see opera. Opera! That was the worst of it. That's what they'd been to see? Fat ladies and that bloody awful warbling that made Cat sick to the pit of his stomach. He hated opera like he hated Manchester United.

Opera! It made him livid as a wound. And it was the opera more than the fact that a cop was knobbing his daughter and a scuzball was seeing to his wife that had worked him up to fever pitch, angry beyond. So it was five minutes to sort-out-time. He was about to send out gilt-edged invitations to his revenge party. But first he was going to souse his cortical stalk in alcohol, give himself a foggy, moody anger which made him more dangerous than a myopic pit-adder in a corner. By the time he'd crunched his favourite crankshaft handle into the loan shark's skull a dozen times or more he'd have a head like a ripe plum, purple and ready to burst. Cat liked the crankshaft handle, it handled easy as a pool cue but had a good weight to it. He walked out of the door and the barman, Maston, knew that Cat was steaming mad about something or other. He'd even forgotten his gas mask.

The four of them knew he was coming and had spent the afternoon making preparations. They had set the Cat Trap with great delicacy, not that he was meant to be caught without pain. The bastard had it coming to him.

The plot had been hatched at the opera, appropriately enough, during the interval in Janacek's 'From the House of the Dead'. Cat's wife, Prudence, was pointing out that the old Czech composer only got started when most people would have been packing it in. Martin added his fourpenn'orth and impressed them all with the fact that he could remember the name of the woman (Kamila Stosslova – not an easy one to remember over a white wine spritzer) who was forty years younger than Janacek, and married, but who drew out of him these words – and Martin said them, word perfectly, 'Wherever there is warmth of pure sentiment, sincerity, truth, and ardent love in my compositions, you are the source of it.'

The three listeners sighed with this, even Stumpy who usually guarded against sentiment. He couldn't afford too much fellow-feeling in his line of business – the sort of usury where the annual percentage rate was over a thousand per cent, and involved putting the squeeze on old biddies who would rather sell the thin blue rivulets of blood in their veins than get into debt. It was the way they'd been brought up. Debt was sin and sin was a signpost to Hell.

Sitting in the busy foyer, replete with melodies and warmed by wine, the four opera-goers felt it a shame that Cat's name had to be invoked, much as bad luck follows running over a toad. He impacted so much on their lives, and, because the two men were scared of him, he surfaced like a Kraken awakening the surface of a pool. His name followed them around like the shadow of a murderer.

His wife mentioned how he'd woken her up once just to force her to listen to him breaking wind. She could have chosen much worse examples of how the man was a savage, but they knew didn't they, they knew the sort of man he was? It didn't need her to point out that Cat was absolutely beyond the pale.

They had set the trip wire half way along the garden path and covered it with some dried leaves. Stumpy hid behind next door's shed (the neighbour, Mrs Stooliss was in on it as well – she'd heard the beatings on Friday nights when Cat's arms hadn't been entirely exhaused by flailing against the police) with a large plank in hand. Martin, risking his career, his pension, a jail sentence – and all for the love of Florence – had a piece of hessian sacking over his head and was busy adjusting the eye holes when he heard the sound of Cat's four-by-four coming up the road. He adjusted the rumpled temples of his mask and checked that he had all the necessaries – baling twine, masking tape, a coil of fishing line with a huge breaking strain, a pair of handcuffs (Army not police issue) and, just in case, a gun.

The vehicle brought a sub-sonic rumble with it up the street. Prudence remembered how Cat had broken her wrist once, snapped it like a twig. Prudence's dry mouth gulped air like a goldfish on a kitchen floor. Another memory of a marriage gone wrong. That dying goldfish, thrashing with its pathetic fins as the life snuffed out.

The door of the Land-Cruiser slammed shut like a thunderclap then Cat opened the front gate as if he was trying to rip it out of the earth. He took four paces forward before the trip wire brought him to the ground. In a dapper movement Stumpy hammered the plank down on the man's back, just one stroke, just enough to wind him, surprise him so that putting on the cuffs was made that much easier. Moving with balletic grace and precision, the two men rolled him over – not without difficulty because all that bulk was made of muscle and gristle and battle-hardened bone. They ran the masking tape over his eyes and bound his ankles with the fishing twine, pausing only to use some squares of newspaper to save the paper roughing up the skin. It was an odd act of consideration, almost of compassion, especially as the two men's hearts were racing, their eyeballs on stalks with the sheer audacity of what they were doing and the recognition that the tremendous musculature and the red-hot anger that was contained within the man's tree stump frame was a mixture as deadly as nitro-glycerine, only more volatile and more explosive. It was also undignified for a man to be lying trussed, gagged and blindfolded on his own front path, especially as his wife and daughter had just arrived with the wheelbarrow to carry him up to the house. The small wheels almost buckled under the weight. Stumpy imagined he saw smoke coming off the limp body like a distress flare or a child's firework.

They carried him to the basement where an Ottoman was ready for him, securely screwed to the floor. They first tied him up with thicker rope, then chained one handcuff to a metal ring set into the floor which they'd concreted in three days previously. They took off his blindfold so that he saw four figures – each sporting joke shop masks. He knew full well who they were but Martin had been reading an Amnesty International report which described ways in which the Iraqi regime broke the spirit of dissidents. Confusion and sleep deprivation were high on the list of preferred torture options. Beyond the figures and right in front of Cat stood a hi-fi. One of the figures, Minnie Mouse, moved over to the hi-fi and switched on the CD function. The melodies of Mozart's 'The Magic Flute' filled the room stereophonically . . .

All this happened three years ago. The Cat is still in the basement, his muscles atrophied through lack of use so that he looks a broken man. Twice a day he's fed, washed, treated like an invalid. He doesn't struggle anymore, even when it's time to use the bedpan. But the torture continues. Last weekend his wife – whose name now escapes him – bought a boxed set of Verdi operas down at HMV. That should fill the week . . .

No-one in the street mentions Cat. There is a conspiracy of silence which has drawn in everyone in town. Everyone is implicated because everybody chooses to be. The only clue to his existence is the occasional moment when, unguardedly – perhaps while mowing the lawn or trimming the dahlias – a soul might whistle a snatch of 'La Traviata' or 'La Boheme' and his neighbour responds by smiling, knowingly, but without the merest vestige of guilt. You can learn to love opera, eventually. Or so they say.

Change on the Way

If you're blind you can cause absolute bloody mayhem in pubs – and get away with it. So much so that I now see my twin haemorrhages as liberations, licenses to play silly buggers. Well, a man's got to have a bit of fun, inhe? I do love the stunt where I stumble and bump into a loaded table, hear the smash of glass. I did it down the Angel last Saturday night and it was a gas, believe me, 'coz this man was at my throat and ready to pulp me straight off.

'What's wrong with you – are you blind or what?' They say it with a predictability which is positively frightening. This man's voice came at me out of a miasma of hot alcohol, close up to my face. Whisky breath, sandpaper accent.

'I am, actually.'

'What?' This brief blurt of a question brought with it a whiff of hops and a hint of rotten molars. My other senses really are compensating nowadays.

'Blind. I am blind.'

'So where's your white stick and your guide dog?' The man was confused. I could hear the tremolo in his voice – the scared boy in him coming out to play.

At that point – and this always floors them – I opened my eye-box wide as wide can be.

'Look I've got no pupils and no irises just some white jelly. Will that be proof enough – or should I walk into a wall or two just as a clincher?'

That always shuts them up. It sure shut him up and I could hear him back with his mates, saving face. He bought me a drink too and I took the sting out of the situation by promising not to get blind drunk. And the point is this. Some blind people are wind-up merchants same as seeing folk. Stands to reason dunnit?

Not that I was always blind, no sir! It happened in work. Wednesday 7th September 1979 and it felt as if I'd taken half the steelworks in the face. They rebuilt much of it, like building something from a kit but the eyes, well . . .

In the hospital a cavalcade of shrinks helped me deal with my anger and resentment with group therapy and pink pills and psycho-babble until I thought I would go completely doolally and by the time I left the place I was a writhing mess of anger and resentment. It was a place in Surrey, on the edge of a lake and I remember listening to the calls of mandarin ducks and realising that I would never see one again. Much of the rest of that time is blotted out by pain, literally under wraps.

But, miracle of miracles, all that pain and anger dissipated this very lunch time.

I was playing pool, no don't be surprised, it's a skill I have that makes me a good few bob on the q.t. I suppose they think it's dead clever, gauging the geometry of the cushion by the sound of the clicks. And I was on a roll – balls dropping clean into the pockets and I was having this guy on that I could tell the colours of the balls without his help, all I had to do was listen very, very carefully and I could hear the yellow and the green as sounds. The guy swallowed it, hook and line.

It must have been getting on for one o'clock when this girl came in, smelling of patchouli for Chrissake. Patchouli! I hadn't smelled patchouli since the days when I looked like Frank Zappa, gribo days, the fag end of the Sixties. And Patchouli girl just perched up on the bar next to me and ordered a cognac, which in our pub was an event on a par with a Mars landing.

'The fragrance of patchouli has just wafted in on the afternoon air, Brian.'

'How did you know?' asked the woman, in a voice near the twenty five year mark, the accent local – Neath, maybe.

'Oh, a finely trained nose for the exotic, me: a sort of swap I made for the gift of sight.'

'Were you born blind?' she asked in an accent which I narrowed down to Glynneath, more particularly to Cwmgwrach.

Then she held my hand, she held my hand and so help me there was a wave of warmth, exactly like having your body floating in the Mediterranean and we started talking and why on earth she should choose to talk about films with a blind man I do not know but we were soon talking about all the films I'd seen over the years down the Rex and up the Scala and we were talking Gregory Peck and Ava Gardner and she told me how she was unattached and I told her about my mother who made the best floral arrangements in Resolven and we were on a roll, coasting along, like cyclists in the sea breezes of Big Sur, a Californian sort of afternoon, you know.

I asked if I could walk her home but she explained that she had come on her bike which was chained outside.

'No problem,' I said with a jauntiness born of a good few beers. I had spent a good many neck oil vouchers seeing as I'd only come out for a half. 'You go on the handlebars.'

'But you're blind,' she said.

'And pissed,' I said, 'so that's a double jeopardy.'

'All right. Take me to Comet Street,' and she started yelling orders about avoiding potholes and I was shouting that I knew a short cut behind the bungalows near the arch and I could hear that song 'Raindrops Keep Falling On My Head' but when it came to swinging us both through the gate – and we were fair zipping along by the point – with my memory working double overtime it turned out that the field had just been ploughed. We splotched down in a muddy puddle and I landed in a cold trench of water and the next thing I knew she was laughing and holding me and when she held me it was, I swear, like a blind person would hold me. I knew then that the smell of mud mixed with patchouli was the sign of big change coming.

Making the Switch

I'd been toying with the idea of transvestism ever since my uncle Dill showed me the frock. We were down the lock-up, where he spent his evenings as a tinkering mechanic, repairing cars, hoovers, pretty much anything that had moving parts. And without a repair manual.

We'd just had the fourth cup of Glengettie when Dill said, 'I've got something to show you, Harry.' His voice was deep, sub-sonic almost, with a gruff edge from years of determined chain smoking. He took me round the back of an old grey filing cabinet. On a hanger was the dress, a lemon affair – from the Fifties maybe.

'Isn't she a corker?' he asked, with a reverence in his voice as if he was talking about a Maserati, his favourite car. I was flummoxed.

'Very nice Dill. Very nice.'

'You can touch it if you like, but you'll have to get the crap off your hands with a dab of Swarfega first.'

I poured out a green glob from the jar, massaged it into my fingers. The next thing I knew I was getting out of my jeans and trying on the dress. It was the right size . . .

'Such silky smooth material,' said Dill. 'I often put it on when I know I'm going to be alone. I'm looking for a pair of heels to go with it. There was a lovely pair in Barnados but they were much too small for me.'

After I'd changed back again we had another cup of tea. I didn't say anything about the dress. I was stunned. Dill talked about the Rugby World Cup and how the Welsh renaissance was a long time coming. He talked about secondhand cars and reminisced about a motorcycling holiday on the back of a vintage Norton. At half-nine I walked home. In bed I felt myself running my hands across the duvet, smoothing it, palping it, but it wasn't as smooth as the dress. It just wasn't.

I returned the following Thursday. Dill was mending a lawn mower which had some wire coiled around the blades. The smell of pulverised grass cuttings was incongruous among the diesel oil, the smell of metal filings, exotic almost. I helped him lift out the blades. Dill unwound the wire from the flywheel.

'That's the bugger,' he said.

Later, as we cracked open a new packet of Bensons Dill leaned towards me, con-spir-atorial.

'I called in the Oxfam shop over the weekend. Got myself an amazing feather boa, a tenpenny bargain. Look!'

It was a boa-and-a-half. A real Barbara Cartland number, Dill draped it around his neck.

'It clashes with your overalls,' I said, and laughed fit to burst.

I started paying attention to women's fashions after that. I even found myself enjoying Cosmopolitan down at the barbers'. When Stan started cracking jokes I let him have it.

'Clam it Stan. I'm just swotting up to be a transvestite.'

He didn't know how to take that but laughed it off. He offered to give me a demi-semi perm. 'Just give me a number two razor, above the ears, square at the back.'

Secretly the idea of a perm, especially a demi-semi perm – whatever that was – thrilled me. But my image in work would be scuppered. Being a physiotherapist to one of the best rugby teams in Wales and going bouffant don't mix. The boys in the squad wouldn't be too happy having their groin muscles massaged by Danny la Rue. Apart from the scrum-half, maybe, but that's another story. A scandal would erupt, as big as the payola one which rocked the club last season. I'd be out on my nose. My badly broken nose, probably.

Dill's enthusiasm was catching. I was down the lock-up twice a week. We even started working in our show clothes. I ordered some shoes from a shop in London, 'Male-Order.' Dill had brought a wardrobe, second-hand and he'd excelled himself by getting hold of a full length mirror.

'We must look like a right pair of Charlies,' I suggested.

'Charlenes more like – a little curious in our garb. But wait till you see what I've got.'

He disappeared behind the filing cabinet. After a few minutes of rustling Dill reappeared. He was wearing a wedding trousseau, veil and all.

'Where on earth did you get that,' I asked him, astonished and impressed.

'Bessie got married in it.'

Bessie was his wife, of thirty years standing. A real poppet. Heart of gold.

'What if she finds out?'

'She won't. She's away at some Liberal do in Eastbourne.'

He paraded up and down the concrete edge of the oil-pit. I clapped, mainly at the sheer audacity of the thing. Dill did a final twirl, got changed, and suggested we should retire to the 'Cow and Snuffers' for a jar.

The following Saturday I woke up with a burning flame inside, like an oxy-acetylene, or an arc-lamp. I got dressed double-quick and drove straight into town. The lady behind the counter at Dorothy Perkins looked as if she'd been night-clubbing, her eyes half-open.

'I want to open a charge account,' I said.

'Just fill in one of these forms. They're very popular. We had a run on them before Christmas. I'm sure your lady friend will be thrilled . . . '

'Madam,' I said, fixing her with a gimlet eye. 'This account's for me. Now, could you direct me to the lingerie section?'

She pointed her finger, her mouth agape.

That day I wore the pink polka dot dress of freedom. After lunch I went to see the Pontypool match. And stole the show more completely than the winning try. Barratt out to Williams, who pushed it over within a whisker of the corner flag. A little corker. Like me, up there on the stand, clapping the skin off my palms, in my very highest heels.

Teeth

Cled's dental fillings were going to put him in the Crazy House. No doubt about that. Oh no! Especially after he shut the door on his good friend Marty – The Source Of All Matters Medical And In Particular Things Carcinogenic and Otherwise Harmful – after he'd paid a surprise visit. Marty'd only been around at Cled's long enough to drink a cup of green tea and eat a date cake but it was enough time to deliver a mini-lecture which not so much put the frighteners on Cled as scared him out of his skin.

Marty stood near the window with a demonic light burning in his eyes as he regaled him with his latest discoveries which he had culled from journals as learned as 'The Lancet' and organs as august as the 'Daily Star'.

' . . . And so, every time we take anything orally, when we smoke, drink a drink or chew a morsel, the friction and general rubbing down of an old filling creates mercuric oxide gas which then poisons us slowly and there's sod all anyone can do about this sort of poisoning. You can have them out mind – but that involves locking off the throat and having an air-line running to the patient and another running to the dentist and swear-to-God when they get round to disposing of the old fillings they have those guys in biochemical warfare suits turning up at the surgery and . . . ' Marty took in a huge gulp of air before continuing ' . . . what's more those old fillings when they were put in place probably expanded to fill the tooth so fast that the tooth was probably cracked beyond redemption in the process.'

'Don't choke on your date cake,' said Cled with more than a twist of citric venom, his mind a swirl of poisonous vapours. He knew the potency of mercury ever since a school chum, Eifion Prosser (now on a long stretch in Long Larten nick – no surprises there) had poured mercuric nitrate into an aquarium full of guppies and luminous neon tetras.

The fish had all swum backwards for a few seconds before flipping over and floating to the top of the tank, the poison so effective that the surface was soon a scum of brightly coloured fish.

Marty's scaremongering had the desired effect. Cled's tongue snaked around both rows of teeth, feeling where the fillings were. He had more than a few. Marty was not only a walking rag-bag of medical info; he was a terrible hypochondriac. With this in mind, Cled once fixed him a meal of pheasant in a 'Benylin' sauce. 'The gentle flavours of the cough medicine enhance the dry quality of the game,' said Cled as he brought in the accompanying vegetables. They had both laughed heartily when they served up that one. But one thing was true. Marty talked about ailments and, sure as eggs is eggs, Cled then promptly displayed the symptoms.

Years ago Cled had heard how a friend of the family's, approaching his twenty first birthday had a very special present from his dentist father. The father'd taken out all his teeth – 'saving a fortune in future dental fees, son' and fitting him out with a new set of dentures. Apparently he'd made the dental plate on the sly, using the impression the son had made in a piece of simnel cake, used subtle subterfuge to have things ready for the big day. The poor boy couldn't even blow out his own candles, making a horrible slurping sound as he tried, the sound of a B-movie alien slurping human skin.

Cup of teeth-staining espresso by his side, Cled started brisk work on the day's crossword, but found that the usual ten minutes it took to complete stretched to twenty as his mind drifted. He imagined the answers to some dental trade magazine crossword. 'Root canal.' 'Amalgam.' 'Incisor.' And then those words that summoned up the Gallipoli of the gums. 'Halitotic.' 'Gingivitis.' And 'caries' which, to his younger self, had sounded very much like cavies, or guinea pigs, and he had decided that there simply couldn't be a mouth disease more terrifying than having guinea pigs in the gob – adult ones leaving dabs of fur on the roof of the mouth and hardly any space to breathe, or – more horrible still – baby guinea pigs, like blind worms squeezed out from the between the gums, like pathetic pink maggots emerging. Had Buñuel been into guinea pigs this was a sequence from the film he might have made. Cutting-edge-of-nightmare-stuff.

Cled focused his mind once again. 'Novocaine.' 'Floss.' 'Fluoride.' 'Brace.' The words came thick and fast. And phrases. 'Long in the tooth.' 'A tooth for a tooth.' 'An eye tooth for an eye tooth.' And worst of all, vagina dentata, which was enough of an image to pull his scrotum in tight against his body wall.

Cled hadn't realised he carried so much of a dental lexicon around with him. He certainly couldn't understand why it was necessary to spend three years doing a dentistry degree when his grandfather, a feisty man even in his early nineties, used to yank out his rotten teeth with no anaesthetic and nothing more surgical than the door handle, a length of string and his wife's co-operation. With a shivery spine, Cled remembered one of those extractions, his grandmother standing on one side of the door, waiting for the shouted instruction.

'Tynnwch y drws, Lizzie,' and she'd pull with all the vestigial might of her atrophied and ancient arms. There was the look of terrified failure when she realised that she simply didn't have the strength any more, the door yanked only a few inches open, the pained puppy-like yelping of her husband on the other side. 'You do it Cled, before he bleeds to death.' That was the sort of thing that crept into his nightmares. Lest he bleed to death. He closed the door, looped the string twice around his right arm and took a fast start away from the door as if he was breaking away from running blocks. The impetus was enough to uproot the tooth, but caught his grandfather off balance so that the old man banged his head against the door-frame before slumping to the floor. They found him sitting there like a cartoon drunk, the sort that has stars whizzing around his skull. 'Mae e mas,' he said, showing the rusty red stump and the tooth like one of a set found on a head-hunter's necklace. He handed it to his grandson with a mischievous look in his eyes, then said, 'Go on, put it under your pillow and see what you get.' Ripping off the tooth fairy gave Cled a sleepless night but not so sleepless that he didn't fail to see the tooth fairy creeping in and putting a golden guinea under his head. A guinea. Now that really was allowing for inflation.

Cled started to notice other people's teeth almost to the point of distraction. A woman in the fruitshop displayed a dentition as jagged as a great white shark's as she rolled a piece of coriander in cellophane wrap. A care in the community type – a slipper shuffler out in all weathers – mouthed silent words so that he most resembled a goldfish. Try saying the name 'Bob' without making a sound and you'll get some idea of where the goldfish comparison comes from.

He wished he could sometimes just go up to complete strangers and peer deep into their buccal cavities. He longed with a desire almost sweatily carnal to own one of those small dental mirrors so that he could examine the backs of their mouths, to perform acts of unutterable intimacy.

A girl at the Safeway counter had a gold filling like a Romany princess. A woman at the bus queue had such ill fashioned dentures that they seemed moulded out of a child's 'Play-dough', squidgy and garish, the fake gums the colour of old telephone boxes. And at the leisure centre he spotted a boy with such bad decay that there were black stripes of rotten enamel against a backdrop of yellowy gnashers: his mouth looked like a piano keyboard. Cled balanced the horror of this image by remembering the smiles of a procession of Miss Worlds – their perfect smiles the perfect complement to the desire to be a hairdresser and work for world peace.

Cled's solitary act of violence against a fellow human being had ended with a lot of teeth. The love of his life, Marsha, had been on a business trip to Bangkok where she'd met a fellow lecturer who serenaded her with Persian poetry. When she came home she admitted her infidelity and said she'd have to decide between the two of them and let him know by phone on Saturday morning – by phone for Chrissake!

The call never came, so he sprinted to the station and caught a train where he was serenaded by a jazz clarinettist – but that's another story – and when Cled arrived in Bath he was a little the worse for wear and copious swigs of Jamaican overproof rum and coke. He poured himself into a taxi, staring out at the street scenes without registering a single thing. When he arrived at the love nest (which he had helped to feather incidentally) the lovebirds were just coming down the stairs, each with an overnight bag in hand.

He hadn't understood the expression 'to see red' until that very microsecond when his vision was a wash of crimson.

Cled called his rival a few choice unpleasant things before swinging a crunching fist which connected with his mouth. There was a spray of blood and dislodged teeth, nine teeth in total, which lay on the pavement in a bright red pool which darkened and became viscous even as Cled surveyed his bloody handiwork. It looked like a black pudding in the making, a mess of black flecked with white.

Marsha cradled her lover's pain-racked head in her arms, comforting the man who ululated with pain on the pavement. Cled's ex (he knew there was little chance of reparation after this – he wasn't stupid) had only time, to tell him, with a complete and devastating sense of irony, 'You know if you hadn't done that I'd have come back to you.' She spat out the words even as her man spat out another tooth which skittered across the kerbside and dropped into a drain.

Marty's words had really unsettled him. Cled dwelled on the possibility that he was being slowly poisoned by his teeth and the words 'nothing they can do' resonated in his head like a Balinese gong. His whole life was reflected in his teeth – the slight mustard staining of that period in his life when he could have smoked for Wales; the dog tooth that had been taken out when he was seven, leaving a gap he could whistle through like a top shepherd, able to work a collie in a fog. And there was the period when he was still knee high to a dandelion when he found himself a lab rat under the orthodontist-from-hell, who chose to tackle an overhang up top, an overbite, by creating a brace which was a real sadist's masterwork, an architecture of spokes and chrome bars which retained tiny souvenirs of every meal. It irritated Cled so much it finally ended up joining the discarded cycles and mangled shopping trolleys at the bottom of the canal, scything into the water with barely a plop.

Clem stared at his mouth in the mirror – the fleshy lips that might have been arcs peeled off some exotic fruit and the slightly vampiristic dog teeth which looked as if they might better grace a hyena. He was an inveterate meat eater, a tearer of flesh and a grinder of gristle and felt sure that his incisors had been growing with each and every sirloin that he tackled, every Barnsley chop and saltmarsh lamb a micron or two's worth of growth.

Growing up, he'd robbed the tooth fairy of a good few bob and, because his mother'd told him the sprite was only half an inch long, he'd actually felt sorry for the little imaginary bugger, saw it clutching an outsize molar as it tried to achieve take off from the pillow with its wings no bigger than a bumble bee's. Must have been a couple of quid he'd left in exchange over the years. He'd often pondered where did the fairy get hold of cash, human money at that? Borrowed it off a changeling, perhaps?

One morning, that same week, Cled woke up and imagined himself as a giant tooth, a conceit less interesting, a metamorphosis less telling than Kafka's beetle. Another day he imagined ghoulish after-hours work at the crematorium, feverish assistants freeing the gold teeth before the cadavers hit meltdown behind the purple screens. Cled thought about the forty seven teeth a mosquito possesses. He thought of tusks and fangs and molars. He day dreamed about the advert for the Colgate 'ring of confidence'. His mind conjured up fashion models with rows of teeth like parched headstones in the

Mojave desert and Cled realised that he was in danger of losing it, such was his fixation.

As he walked down to the surgery he replayed the scene from 'Marathon Man' which put a whole heap of people off getting their teeth fixed. The mind's celluloid flickered: Dustin Hoffman in the chair, Laurence Olivier the dentist with a Nazi past.

He turned into a leafy suburb where the light breaking through the cascades of laburnum created a patchwork of lemon dappled light and dark shadows. He walked up the drive of a huge house with six bay windows and a castellated roof. Plenty of money in teeth, thought Cled, who walked with steady resolve in each step.

The nurse gave him an injection which felt as if his cheek had been dipped in liquid nitrogen. The dentist who then appeared reminded Cled of the image of a serial killer he had in a book called the 'Murderer's Who's Who' – a man called Laurence Dodd – a dastardly torturer who'd trained in vivisection labs before turning to more human experiments.

'Open wide,' said Laurence Dodd, starting up a drill which whined ferociously like a tiny demented hornet.

'You want them all out. You're sure now.' But with the rubber grip wedging his mouth wide, and his jaw wired open, Cled wouldn't have been able to say anything to the contrary even had he wanted to.

'You can leave us now nurse. I may be a while.' As the blonde assistant left through the swing doors the dentist swapped the gleaming stainless steel tools for a Victorian array of pliers and rusty drills from a battered Gladstone bag at his side.

'Right,' he said, 'let's get down to it.' He winked with a leer at Cled whose heart was close to spasm.

'Open wide,' said the dentist, as Cled realised that the nurse had only anaesthetised one half of his face.

'Open wide.'

The Stuff of Fairy Tales

Depending on how you look at them magpies can look like speeded-up butterflies, or exploded sheets of black and white paper but Herringway, better known as Herring, potent gamekeeper of the high hills, looked on them as total enemies. He was a gamekeeper of shoot 'em, trap 'em and put-strychnine-down-for-them School of Gamekeeping. He hated magpies more than he hated children, and that was saying something. In his moorland fief, halfway between Blaenycwm and Cefn yr Asyn war was waged on a daily basis. Not a day went by without the silence on the tops being shattered by shotgun blasts. The bloody, mangled gleanings from the pole trap and dead things aplenty gave the place the look of an open graveyard, carnage H.Q. Animals and birds, other than magpies copped it of course, but this comprehensive carnage was justified by the hatred which drove the small, bullet shaped man so furiously.

Herring made human contact on Fridays only, when the squire, Trelarchey, came up the hill to dole out the week's wage. The diminished aristocrat would often have to drop to all fours to cope with the final incline of Fochriw. Herring, an observer without pity, would impassively watch the old man struggling. The ritual which followed was simple. Trelarchey would enquire after the health of the birds, then enquire after Herring's health. Then a brass counting box would appear and the money slowly, so creakingly slowly, counted. The keeper would pocket it quickly with a ferret hand, knowing that he had little to spend it on apart from the instruments of war against the magpies. But that was satisfaction enough.

The rest of the time Herring was claustrophobically alone in his bitter countryside. The seasons rolled by, taking the slates off the roof, drifting hawthorn snow over the hedges and placing rafts of ice on the ponds and stilling the brooks. Summer, when it came, was a curtailed affair, bringing extra light but little heat to the tops. There were sun traps, it has to be said, but Herring shunned these. His main task was rearing grouse, although he was also expected to keep the tracks and roads in good repair. These tasks gave him a wage, but the genocide of magpies, well now, that gave him prime satisfaction, naked and good.

Even in his remote empire Herring would be forever on the alert, watchful lest anyone see the rituals he had concocted for his bird-enemies. He would suspend a dead magpie between two saplings and slash at the join of wing and body. It was a bloodily frenzied, demon possessed hack-hacking. He would burn the bodies but the wings he would take up onto the high tops. He would drop one here, another there over a huge area and it would give him pleasure to chance upon a wing. It would make his day. In his mind, dark and sullen as it usually was there would flash one brilliant, searing image. He would carpet the very moor with feathers and wings, the heather would be suffocated by the weight of black, grey and white feathers. This was his grail, his fortification, his doom.

One day Herring woke earlier than usual. Dawn was only just cutting through the clouds, a silk swirl of red and darker. Some pheasants, displaced banshees called outside. Their percussive calls diffused across the heather, breaking finally on beds of cloudberries. The keeper padded across to the scullery where he fastidiously scrubbed his hands, careful to wash away every small crumb of bird-blood. Morning toilet over he would drink a cup of warm water and take a lump of bread.

He stood on the cottage threshold and called his dog, but he didn't come. He was probably still making his way back from courting. A smile, a line, broke out on the man's austere face as he remembered how Dog had served three bitches in one evening describing an arc of what must be thirty miles. There had been hell to pay. Crossing the yard Herring shouted again, a great stentorian bellow which broadened out into a great sheet and spread thinly across Foel Fadog and Y Gallt. One farmer threatened Herring with a shotgun, but Herring unblinkingly lifted his own shotgun, took studious aim at the farmer's eyes and saw him coursing down the field like a hare.

The keeper enjoyed his morning's round of the traps. He was the gaunt avenger, delivering death – that's the way he saw it – delivering death not relieving suffering. The distinction. He dispatched rabbits with a deadening blow from his knobkerrie. Owls and buzzards with their legs broken and smashed by the cutting steels of pole-traps flapped pointlessly, not for take-off. A fifty-nine year-old man with a marble heart would kill their dream of flying. But this morning was to be different.

Herring climbed over the bottom stile of White Mynd field and crossed the brook, studded with the yellow heads of marsh marigolds. A grasshopper warbler turned the little fishing reel of his song in a tight jungle of brambles, but Herring registered neither flowers nor bird. The bestiary of his mind was confined to the birds he had to rear and these marched in Pied Piper procession, one red grouse after another and in the rear were those that tried to kill his grouse – hooked beaks and fox skulls, weasel eyes and talons gripping grouse-chicks, a light rain of tiny feathers, blood bespattered. These were the other images massed inside the heavy dome of his skull. Then Herring heard the flute.

The notes of the flute were shrill and wove a frantic, dislocated melody. Herring recognised this as the song of pain and started loping, then running down the path, towards the sound. Dog was lying on the ground, one leg almost wrenched out of the hip-socket with the effort of trying to free itself from the snare. Herring froze, uncertain of the best thing to do. His thoughts accelerated, up a cog, shifting gear. The dog would probably survive amputation, be able to walk after a fashion, that tendency to topple almost humorous. But he would no longer be a working dog. A decision was lost somewhere in the whorl, sometimes glimpsed. Time froze. The decision then came to rest.

He cut a short length of twig and wedged it behind the dog's molars, choking it, almost. Wiping the knife on the seat of his moleskins Herring felt confident about the sharpness of the blade, stropped religiously as it was against grey stone every evening. With one hand he forced the length of wood back towards the seal of the dog's lips, pushing the dog itself back into the hedge. It jerked with the electricity of pain. Herring worked with the dexterity of surgeon, pushing the blade into the flesh and cutting around the dexterity and purpose. The dog flopped, the knife stopped. The dog was exhausted, its blood a dark stream. The stump-wound was sealed with a piece of baling twine, the keeper pulling with every ounce to staunch the flow of blood.

The dog survived, but Herring's cruelty did not, as would happen in any fairy tale ending. Over the next few days down came the pole traps, up came the mole-traps, gin traps were dismantled, snares were tightened for the very last time. It wasn't that sunshine lit up the sides of Herring's face from then on, or that orchids suddenly flowered in the back yard between the cottage and the lean-to. But Herring began to admire magpies, began to see them as exploded paper or butterflies of a bright, whirring brilliance.

Tom's Wild Present

Fran Wagstaffe had decided on an exhilaratingly exotic anniversary present for her husband Tom while he was away at a sales convention. Tom sold vacuum cleaners with a vengeance. Inevitably he would come home with the top salesman award of a pewter vacuum cleaner – one sixth life size – and a pair of tickets to fly to Miami. So Fran got on the phone.

Good steel erectors aren't easy to come by and after a great many calls in vain to weary voiced men who tut-tutted and said 'we don't handle that sort of thing, luv,' Fran had ended up seeking help from a neglected cousin who worked in the trade.

Cousin Clarence put her on to the firm that built the cage in the garden in next to no time. Fran's neighbours, who'd missed out on their true vocations in intelligence gathering and surveillance, watched all goggle-eyed as the eight elegant arcs of serious metal were hoisted into place and slotted into the concrete slab base. Mrs Gratings, from next door-but-two summoned up the necessary temerity to ask what it was exactly – too big for a greenhouse frame, too, well, permanent for a pergola.

'It's an anniversary present for Tom, Mrs Gratings. A small gift to mark ten years which have been haunted by happiness. It's not many women who have been rewarded as much as I have by the institution of marriage.'

Fran was laying it on with a trowel. What was more she was lying through her teeth. She wasn't happy and that was that. Fran, jolted by this fact, decided to confide in her neighbour what was going in the cage, just to test her reaction.

'I'm getting him a black panther.'

'Oh that's nice,' said Mrs Gratings, not altogether sure she'd heard correctly. A black panther? Surely not. Not in Laburnum Close, where house prices never went down.

That afternoon the local telephone exchange was close to meltdown as the neighbourhood watch organiser, Mabel Hurd, phoned the woman next door but three, Mrs Gaskets, who, in turn, thought the event noteworthy enough to ring up relatives overseas. The Chinese whispers had it that that Mrs Wagstaff in Number twenty three was going to breed panthers, yes, really, Dillwyn. Yes, panthers! That's it, like a black leopard. I ask you. What is the world coming to?

The man at the council offices filled in the form as glass beads of sweat bore out chaos theory on his pebbledashed brow. The unfortunate bureaucrat wasn't too au fait with the intricacies of the Control of Dangerous Animals Act but it was written into his job description so he had to brazen it out. So he filled in the details of Mrs Francesca Whitemore's black panther and took the completed licence form to be counter-signed by his boss.

'And this woman's giving her husband a whopping great circus animal as an anniversary present?'

'As a surprise.'

'Big surprise. Has she any previous experience of keeping animals this big?'

'Oh yes!' said the toadying assistant with alacrity. 'She had one fifteen years ago. She and her late husband kept one in the grounds of a factory he managed somewhere out Wolverhampton way. Said it was better security than a dozen Rottweilers.'

'Her late husband?'

'That's what she said.'

The boss counted to three after the assistant shut the door before reaching for the desk drawer where he kept a dog-eared copy of 'Health and Efficiency' and a tiny silver flask of the good stuff. As he took a small swig of Irish whisky he thought of the black panther, its eyes glowing in some forest of the night.

The animal arrived the day before Tom was due to return. An

orange van came up the driveway and a man with a squint asked, matter of factly, 'Where do you want him then?' Fran almost said 'Oh just put him in the kitchen and I'll sort him out later . . . ' but thought better of it. This was after all a dangerous animal. Frank took the man out into the garden where the roses were in full bloom. The man's eyes alit on the cage.

'It's a beaut. Best I've seen in a long while. It could do with a log or two or summat so it can work its claws. But the run, that's the thing, it's what a panther most needs. Plenty of room to prowl and pad around in. That way they don't build up a head of anger.'

'Anger?'

The man ignored Fran's question and barked at an assistant who was smoking a cigarette in the cab. He sauntered over, looking sheepish. He also had a squint and had to focus hard to take in the scene. Fran imagined them to be a father and son team: something something and son, panther delivering a speciality. Fran heard a snorting sound in the cage – a sound disdainful of all the petttinesses of man – that sort of snort.

Moving the panther into the cage was straightforward. They backed the van up to the door of the cage, slid back three pairs of bolts, lifted the heavy metal bar of the cage door and the animal poured itself into its new home, a dark shadow of its own self. Its lemon eyes stared straight ahead, other than when a startled collared dove caromed out of the laurel hedge. The heavy black head, seemingly sculpted out of ebony, nodded and lolled as it investigated the cage, looking for faults lines in the steel bars.

The panther snarled at the assistant as he lit a cigarette, flicking out a flame from a brass cigarette lighter. The assistant bared his teeth back at the panther. Fran laughed nervously.

'He's not scared of cats, my boy,' said the father, wreathed in pride.

'Have you got enough food, missus?' he continued, while Fran filled in details and added her signature to the form he held out on a clipboard.

Fran had plenty of food. She had been to the wholesale meat market only that morning, where she had traded hard for a thirty kilo sack of steaks. The butcher threw in a tray of faggots. Tom liked a nice faggot supper.

Fran pulled back the net curtains so that she could enjoy an uninterrupted view across the lawn. As she did her ironing, she found her arm motions mirroring that of the black cat in the garden, back and fore, back and fore. Its laser beam eyes seemed to know what she was doing, could smell the starched whiteness of the fresh laundry. The animal could smell her bones and the flesh wrapped around their white crunchiness through the window glass. She felt sure of it.

After she had put the shirts on their hangers she poured himself a measure of cherry vodka and started to read the dossier the delivery men had left her. It didn't add up to what one might call an instruction manual, more a package of photocopied bits and pieces, culled from zoo yearbooks, newspapers, learned journals and mammal books. Fran learned that a panther was called a puma in the States and that its name came, straightforwardly, from the Greek, panther.

She found a biro and wrote out a short list of names for their new pet, if you could call it that. She pored over the list for a few minutes, then took a long sip of the vodka and plumped for Dark Star. Yes, Dark Star. A star that sucks in light.

As she read her way deeper into panther territory her neighbours were doing the rounds, gathering names on a petition against keeping wild animals in the neighbourhood. 'Our children won't be safe.'

The panther prowled its inner landscape – startling miniature deer at waterholes, bite-sized living morsels which barely filled the bloody clamp of its jaws. Chittering parakeets alerted the whole of the jungle to its presence: wild pigs ploshed away over waterlogged root systems, their sophisticated snouts sensing this darkest of dangers. Its pads swallowed the weight of the sound it made as it moved around, the suspension springs of its sleek musculature absorbing the impact of its panthery progress. Here was an animal that knew the core of the night as its true habitat.

Fran pored over distribution maps and realised for the first time that the panther was the Indian name for the leopard. To think she'd bought the animal without knowing the etymology of its name! Panther, a perfect name, a name that trod around the tongue on kitten pads. Fran read about its conservation status, its breeding success in zoos from San Diego to Berlin. She traced the shape of game reserves with her fingers, on maps which were concertinaed with age. In these remote reserves the panther maintained a precarious clawhold because of hunting and habitat decay. Fran felt the guilt of her species and a warm rush from the vodka.

As she retired for the night Fran thought she caught a glimpse of The Other Woman, arms wrapped around Tom's shoulders in a photograph on the bedside cabinet. It was an eidolon-image that disappeared in the time it took Fran to blink. She laid the photograph in a cradle of underwear in a drawer. Face downwards.

The following evening Fran heard the purr of the Volvo as it turned up the drive. Tom came through the front door bearing a bouquet of white flowers and the expected vacuum cleaner statuette. Fran kissed Tom wetly, falsely on the lips. She ushered him onto the patio.

'I've got a surprise for you. Shut your eyes.'

She led him, step by step down to the garden path. He kept his eyes shut, and winced a little as he remembered a line from a telephone conversation they'd had earlier in the week. The bit where he told her he'd left his American Express card under the clock in the dining room and that she really should buy herself something nice. He imagined her nursing the plastic to the point of meltdown in a boutique too exquisite to even have a name.

Fran threw a switch which brought up the swimming pool lights, the lawn bright as a floodlit football pitch, the wavy shadows reflected off the pool making the cage and its brooding contents seem chimerical. A dislocated head, a movement here, a triangle of ear over there.

'What is it?' asked Tom, reaching for a cigarette in the breast pocket of his shirt.

'It is a cage. What's in it is the right question.'

'What's in it?' asked Tom with a note of weariness.

The panther was wide awake. It seemed to be permanently awake and as the two crossed the lawn towards the cage it growled like a cartoon tiger. The one in the 'Jungle Book'. Khan.

Fran walked right up to the steel bars. Tom lagged behind, understandably timorous, even to the point of shivering a little. He lagged a good five steps behind his wife.

'It's a panther.

'That's just what I was just thinking.'

'It's a present – for the man who's got everything.'

'What will the neighbours say?' said Tom, eyeing the big cat, which met his gaze.

'Nothing whatsoever if you walk it down the road on a leash. They'll be too petrified to do so much as squawk.'

The panther showed off its perfect incisors, rolling back its upperlip to reveal flesh-tearing teeth if ever there were. Tom lit a cigarette. Lots of people smoked when in the presence of a panther, even when it was contained within struts of high tensile steel. The panther was power.

'Only kidding,' said Fran.

Tom looked perplexed.

'About taking it out on a leash. It would eat you alive.' She hugged her husband in a reassuring embrace.'

'It's a fine animal and, as presents go, one of the best,' said Tom, his head veiled in a purple haze of fag smoke.

'And a bargain to boot . . . '

Tom didn't ask. He couldn't think straight. The panther hypnotised him with eyes that burned with sharp colour and enmity. Dark Star could see the small animal of fear within him, even as his wife scanned his face, looking for more approval.

'What do you think?'

'It's a great present, a fine animal.'

In the morning she showed him how to clean the cage. Fran and Tom shared all the domestic tasks, the sort of model behaviour you'd expect from an ideal couple. Fran showed him how to segregate the panther in one half of the cage so they could clean out the dung and any meaty remains. Once she'd established her husband's confidence she left him to it, shovel in hand, heart in mouth.

As she walked up the crazy-paving she patted the three bolts in her jacket pocket. The bolts that separated the two halves of the cage. She wasn't having any husband of hers playing around with a floosie.

Fran switched on the kettle and then the transistor radio. It was the King of Blarney, Terry Wogan. She turned up his velveteen voice – the essence of Dublin stout – turned it right up. She did not hear the sounds that rent the sedate suburban air, failed to hear the marrow crunching conclusion of the briefest of hunts.

Terry was discussing the secrets of maintaining a successful marriage. Fran had a tip she'd like to share with wives everywhere. It was the way to a man's heart, a short cut, through his stomach, through his very entrails.

Outside, the garden, marooned in mid morning heat, was shocked by birdsong.